Baby Steps to
MARRIAGE

A brand-new duet by
RITA® Award-winning author Barbara Hannay

*Pregnancy is never predictable, and these two
stories explore the very different experiences of
two friends, Mattie and Lucy. Follow their steps to
marriage in these two very special deliveries.*

Expecting Miracle Twins
Mattie Carey has put her dreams of finding Mr. Right
aside to be her best friends' surrogate.
Then Jake Devlin steps into her life. He's cheeky,
charming, intriguing and gorgeous—
but it's *so* not the right time for her to fall in love....
September 2009

This month:
The Bridesmaid's Baby
Old friends Will Carruthers and Lucy McKenty
are thrown together again as best man and bridesmaid
at Mattie and Jake's wedding, where
unresolved feelings resurface. Their biological clocks
might be ticking—but a baby together so soon
is the last thing they expect!

"I've been thinking about your baby proposal,' Will said.

"Will, it wasn't a proposal. You know I didn't mean it."

With a distinct lack of haste, he said, "But is it such a bad idea?"

Lucy's mouth fell open. Surely he wasn't serious? "Of course it's a bad idea. It's crazy."

"You really want a baby," he said quietly. "You said so last night, and you're worried you're running out of time."

Now it was Lucy who didn't answer. She couldn't. Her heart had risen to fill her throat. She'd never dreamed for a moment that Will would take her flippant comment even half seriously.

This was her dream—to have Will's baby. Okay, maybe the dream also involved Will falling madly and deeply in love with her, but surely half a dream was better than none?

BARBARA HANNAY

The Bridesmaid's Baby

Baby Steps to
MARRIAGE

HARLEQUIN®

TORONTO • NEW YORK • LONDON
AMSTERDAM • PARIS • SYDNEY • HAMBURG
STOCKHOLM • ATHENS • TOKYO • MILAN • MADRID
PRAGUE • WARSAW • BUDAPEST • AUCKLAND

Recycling programs
for this product may
not exist in your area.

ISBN-13: 978-0-373-17616-8

THE BRIDESMAID'S BABY

First North American Publication 2009.

www.eHarlequin.com

Printed in U.S.A.

Barbara Hannay was born in Sydney, educated in Brisbane and has spent most of her adult life living in tropical north Queensland, where she and her husband have raised four children. While she has enjoyed many happy times camping and canoeing in the bush, she also delights in an urban lifestyle—chamber music, contemporary dance, movies and dining out. An English teacher, she has always loved writing, and now, by having her stories published, she is living her most cherished fantasy. Visit her Web site at www.barbarahannay.com.

Dear Reader,

Just as I finished writing *The Bridesmaid's Baby,* my son's wife gave birth to not one, but two darling girls, Milla and Sophie, identical twins. They are the sweetest little heroines, and their safe arrival was a wonderful thrill for all of our family. For me it was also the perfect way to end my project BABY STEPS TO MARRIAGE.

It's been a huge pleasure for me to write two linked books, and I've had such fun making the dream of a much-wanted baby come true in two quite different stories.

In *The Bridesmaid's Baby,* which is Lucy and Will's story, I had the extra pleasure of sharing Mattie and Jake's wedding with you. It was lovely to revisit the heroine and hero from *Expecting Miracle Twins* and to let you see that the babies, Jasper and Mia, are thriving.

In Lucy and Will's story, I was also able to explore one of my favorite romantic themes—friends to lovers— and to set their romance in the idyllic country town of Willowbank, where Lucy and Will, Mattie, Gina and Tom had all grown up.

As you can imagine, Willowbank and these characters are now incredibly special to me, as are the dear little babies. I can already imagine a new generation…and who knows where that will lead?

I hope you enjoy Lucy and Will's journey to marriage and parenthood.

Warmest wishes,

Barbara

PROLOGUE

A PARTY was in full swing at Tambaroora.

The homestead was ablaze with lights and brightly coloured Chinese lanterns glowed in the gardens. Laughter and the happy voices of young people joined the loud music that spilled out across the dark paddocks where sheep quietly grazed.

Will Carruthers was going away, setting out to travel the world, and his family and friends were sending him off in style.

'Have you seen Lucy?' Mattie Carey asked him as he topped up her wine glass.

'I'm sure I have,' Will replied, letting his gaze drift around the room, seeking Lucy's bright blonde hair. 'She was here a minute ago.'

Mattie frowned. 'I've been looking for her everywhere.'

'I'll keep an eye out,' Will said with a shrug. 'If I see her, I'll let her know you're looking for her.' He moved on to top up other guests' glasses.

But by the time he'd completed a circuit of the big living room and the brightly lit front and side verandas, Will still hadn't seen Lucy McKenty and he felt a vague stirring of unease. Surely she wouldn't leave the party without saying goodbye. She was, in many ways, his best friend.

He went to the front steps and looked out across the garden, saw a couple, suspiciously like his sister Gina and Tom Hutchins, kissing beneath a jacaranda, but there was still no sign of Lucy.

She wasn't in the kitchen either. Will stood in the middle of the room, scratching his head and staring morosely at the stacks of empty bottles and demolished food platters. Where was she?

His brother Josh came in to grab another bottle of bubbly from the fridge.

'Seen Lucy?' Will asked.

Josh merely shook his head and hurried away to his latest female conquest.

A movement outside on the back veranda caught Will's attention. It was dark out there and he went to the kitchen doorway to scan the veranda's length, saw a slim figure in a pale dress, leaning against a veranda post, staring out into the dark night.

'Lucy?'

She jumped at the sound of his voice.

'I've been looking for you everywhere,' he said, surprised by the relief flowing through him like wine. 'Are you OK?'

'I had a headache.' She spoke in a small, shaky voice. 'So I came outside for a bit of quiet and fresh air.'

'Has it helped?'

'Yes, thanks. I feel much better.'

Will moved beside her and rested his arms on the railing, looking out, as she was, across the dark, limitless stretch of the sheep paddocks.

For the past four years the two of them had been away at

Sydney University, two friends from the tiny country town of Willowbank, adrift in a sea of thousands of strangers. Their friendship had deepened during the ups and downs of student life, but now those years were behind them.

Lucy had come home to start work as a country vet, while Will, who'd studied geology, was heading as far away as possible, hurrying overseas, hungry for adventure and new experiences.

'You're not going to miss this place, are you?' she said.

Will laughed. 'I doubt it.' His brother Josh would be here to help their father run Tambaroora. It was the life Josh, as the eldest son, was born to, what he wanted. For Will, escape had never beckoned more sweetly, had never seemed more reasonable. 'I wish you were coming too.'

Lucy made a soft groaning sound. 'Don't start that again, Will.'

'Sorry.' He knew this was a sore point. 'I just can't understand why you don't want to escape, too.'

'And play gooseberry to you and Cara? How much fun would that be?'

The little catch in Lucy's voice alarmed Will.

'But we're sure to meet up with other travellers, and you'd make lots of friends. Just like you always have.'

Lucy had arrived in Willowbank during their last year at high school and she'd quickly fitted into Will's close circle but, because they'd shared a mutual interest in science, she and Will had become particularly good friends, really good friends.

He looked at her now, standing on the veranda in the moonlight, beautiful in an elfin, tomboyish way, with sparkly blue eyes and short blonde hair and soft pale skin. A strange lump of hot metal burned in his throat.

Lucy lifted her face to him and he saw a tear tremble on the end of her lashes and run down her cheek.

'Hey, Goose.' He used her nickname and forced a shaky laugh. 'Don't tell me you're going to miss me.'

'Of course I won't miss you,' she cried, whirling away so he couldn't see her face.

Shocked, Will reached out to her. She was wearing a strapless dress and his hands closed over her bare shoulders. Her skin was silky beneath his hands and, as he drew her back against him, she was small and soft in his arms. She smelled clean like rain. He dipped his head and her hair held the fragrance of flowers.

Without warning he began to tremble with the force of unexpected emotion.

'Lucy,' he whispered but, as he turned her around to face him, anything else that he might have said was choked off by the sight of her tears.

His heart behaved very strangely as he traced the tears' wet tracks with his fingertips. He felt the heated softness of her skin and when he reached the dainty curve of her tear-dampened lips, he knew that he had to kiss her.

He couldn't resist gathering her close and tasting the delicate saltiness of her tears and the sweetness of her skin and, finally, the softness of her mouth. Oh, God.

With the urgency of a wild bee discovering the world's most tempting honey, Will pulled her closer and took the kiss deeper. Lucy wound her arms around his neck and he could feel her breasts pressed against his chest. His body caught fire.

How could this be happening?

Where on earth had Lucy learned to kiss? Like this?

She was so sweet and wild and passionate—turning him on like nothing he'd ever known.

Was this really Lucy McKenty in his arms? His heart was bursting inside his chest.

'Lucy?' Mattie's voice called suddenly. 'Is that you out there, Lucy?'

Light flooded them. Will and Lucy sprang apart and Mattie stared at them, shocked.

They stared at each other, equally shocked.

'I'm sorry,' Mattie said, turning bright red.

'No, it's OK,' they both protested in unison.

'We were just—' Will began.

'Saying goodbye,' Lucy finished and then she laughed. It was a rather wild, strange little laugh, but it did the trick.

Everyone relaxed. Mattie stopped blushing. 'Josh thought you might like to make a speech soon,' she told him.

'A speech?' Will sounded as dazed as he felt.

'A farewell speech.'

'Oh, yes. I'd better say something now before everyone gets too sloshed.'

They went back inside and, with the speed of a dream that faded upon waking, the moment on the veranda evaporated.

The spell was broken.

Everyone gathered around Will and, as he looked out at the sea of faces and prepared to speak, he thought guiltily of Cara, his girlfriend, waiting for him to join her in Sydney. Then he glanced at Lucy and saw no sign of tears. She was smiling and looking like her happy old self and he told himself everything was OK.

Already he was sure he'd imagined the special magic in that kiss.

CHAPTER ONE

THERE were days when Lucy McKenty knew she was in the wrong job. A woman in her thirties with a loudly ticking biological clock should not devote huge chunks of her time to delivering gorgeous babies.

Admittedly, the babies Lucy delivered usually had four legs and a tail, but that didn't stop them from being impossibly cute, and it certainly didn't stop her from longing for a baby. Just one baby of her own to hold and to love.

The longing swept through her now as she knelt in the straw beside the calf she'd just delivered. The birthing had been difficult, needing ropes and a great deal of Lucy's perspiration, but now, as she shifted the newborn closer to his exhausted mother's head, she felt an all too familiar wrench on her heartstrings.

The cow opened her eyes and began to lick her calf, slowly, methodically, and Lucy smiled as the newborn nuzzled closer. She never tired of this miracle.

Within minutes, the little calf was wobbling to his feet, butting at his mother's side, already urging her to join him in a game.

Nothing could beat the joy of new life.

Except…this idyllic scene was an uncomfortable reminder that Lucy had very little chance of becoming a mother. She'd already suffered one miscarriage and now there was a failed IVF treatment behind her. She was sure she was running out of time. The women in her family had a track record of early menopause and she lived with an ever growing sense of her biological clock counting off the months, days, hours, minutes.

Tick, tock, tick, tock.

Swallowing a sigh, Lucy stood slowly and stretched muscles that had been strained as she'd hauled the calf into the world. She glanced through the barn doorway and saw that the shadows had lengthened across the golden grass of the home paddock.

'What's the time?' she asked Jock Evans, the farmer who'd called her in a panic several hours earlier.

Instead of checking his wrist, Jock turned slowly and squinted at the mellowing daylight outside. 'Just gone five, I reckon.'

'Already?' Lucy hurried to the corner of the barn where she'd left her things, including her watch. She checked it. Jock was dead right. 'I'm supposed to be at a wedding rehearsal by half past five.'

Jock's eyes widened with surprise. 'Don't tell me you're getting married, Lucy?'

'Me? Heavens, no.' Peeling off sterile gloves, she manufactured a gaiety she didn't feel. 'Mattie Carey's the lucky girl getting married. I'm just a bridesmaid.'

Again, she added silently.

The farmer didn't try to hide his relief. 'I'm glad you haven't been snapped up. The Willow Creek district can't afford to have you whisked away from us.'

'Well, there's not much chance.'

'Most folks around here reckon you're the best vet we've ever had.'

'Thanks, Jock.' Lucy sent him a grateful smile, but as she went through to the adjoining room to clean up, her smile wavered and then collapsed.

She really, really loved her job, and she'd worked hard for many years before the local farmers finally placed their trust in a mere 'slip of a girl'. Now she'd finally earned their loyalty and admiration and she knew she should be satisfied, but lately this job hadn't felt like enough.

She certainly didn't want to be married to it!

For Will Carruthers, coming home to Willowbank always felt like stepping back in time. In ten years the sleepy country town had barely changed.

The wide main street was still filled with the same old fashioned flower beds. The bank, the council chambers, the post office and the barber shop all looked exactly as they had when Will first left home.

Today, as he climbed out of his father's battered old truck, the familiar landmarks took on a dreamlike quality. But when he pushed open the gate that led to the white wooden church, where tomorrow his best mate would marry one of his oldest friends, he couldn't help thinking that this sense of time standing still was a mere illusion.

The buildings and the landscape might have stayed the same, but the people who lived here had changed. Oh, yeah. Every person who mattered in Will's life had changed a great deal.

And here was the funny thing. Will had left sleepy old Willowbank, eager to shake its dust from his heels and to make his mark on the world. He'd traversed the globe more times than he cared to count, but now, in so many ways, he felt like the guy who'd been left behind.

From inside the church the wailing cries of a baby sounded, a clear signal of the changes that had taken place. Will's sister Gina appeared at the church door, jiggling a howling ginger-headed infant on her hip.

When she saw her brother, her face broke into a huge smile.

'Will, I'm so glad you made it. Gosh, it's lovely to see you.' Reaching out, she beckoned him closer, gave him a one armed hug. 'Heavens, big brother, have I shrunk or have you grown even taller?'

'Maybe the weight of motherhood is wearing you down.' Will stooped to kiss her, then smiled as he studied her face. 'I take that back, Gina. I don't think you've ever looked happier.'

'I know,' she said beaming. 'It's amazing, isn't it? I seem to have discovered my inner Earth Mother.'

He grinned and patted her baby's chubby arm. 'This must be Jasper. He's certainly a chip off the old block.' The baby was a dead ringer for his father, Tom, right down to his red hair. 'G'day, little guy.'

Jasper stopped crying and stared at Will with big blue eyes, shiny with tears.

'Gosh, that shut him up.' Gina grinned and winked. 'You must have the knack, Will. I knew you'd be perfect uncle material.'

Will chuckled to cover an abrupt slug of emotion that had caught him by surprise. Gina's baby was incredibly cute. His skin was soft and perfectly smooth, his eyes bright and clear. There were dimples on his chubby hands and, crikey, dimples on his knees. And, even though he was only four months old, he was unmistakably sturdy and masculine.

'What a great little guy,' he said, his voice rough around the edges.

Gina was watching him shrewdly. 'Ever thought of having a little boy of your own, Will?'

He covered his sigh with a lopsided grin. 'We both know I've been too much of a gypsy.'

Reluctant to meet his sister's searching gaze, Will studied a stained glass window and found himself remembering a church in Canada, where, only days ago, he'd attended the funeral of a work colleague. He could still see the earnest face of his friend's ten-year-old son, could see the pride in the boy's eyes as he'd bravely faced the congregation and told them how much he'd loved his dad.

Hell, if he let himself think about that father and son relationship now, he'd be a mess in no time.

Hunting for a distraction, Will slid a curious glance towards the chattering group at the front of the church. 'I hope I'm not late. The rehearsal hasn't started, has it?'

'No, don't fret. Hey, everyone!' Gina raised her voice. 'Will's here.'

The chatter stopped. Heads turned and faces broke into smiles. A distinct lump formed in Will's throat.

How good it was to see them all again. Tom, Gina's stolid farmer husband, was grinning like a Cheshire cat as he held baby Mia, Jasper's twin sister.

Mattie, the bride-to-be, looked incredibly happy as she stood with her bridegroom's arm about her shoulders.

Mattie was marrying Jake Devlin and Will still couldn't get over the changes in Jake. The two men had worked together on a mine site in Mongolia and they'd quickly become great mates, but Will could have sworn that Jake was not the marrying kind.

No one had been more stunned when Jake, chief breaker of feminine hearts, had fallen like a ton of bricks for Mattie Carey.

One look at Jake's face now, however, and Will couldn't doubt the truth of it. Crikey, his mate had never looked so relaxed and happy—at peace with himself and eager to take on the world.

As for Mattie…Will had known her all his life…but now she looked…well, there was only one word…

Mattie looked *transformed*.

Radiant and beautiful only went part way to describing her.

He couldn't detect any sign that she'd recently given birth to twins—to Gina and Tom's babies, in fact, in a wonderful surrogacy arrangement that had brought untold blessings to everyone involved. Mattie was not only slim once again, but she'd acquired a new confidence that blazed in her eyes, in her glowing smile, in the way she moved.

All this Will noticed as everyone gathered around him, offering kisses, handshakes and backslaps.

'So glad you could make it,' Jake said, pumping his hand.

'Try to keep me away, mate. I'd pay good money to see you take the plunge tomorrow.'

'We're just waiting for the minister and his wife,' Mattie said. 'And for Lucy.'

Lucy.

It was ages since Will had seen Lucy, and he'd never been happy about the way they'd drifted apart, although it had seemed necessary at the time. 'Is Lucy coming to the wedding rehearsal?'

'Of course,' Mattie said. 'Didn't you know? Lucy's a bridesmaid.'

'I thought Gina was the bridesmaid.'

Gina laughed. 'You haven't been paying attention, Will. Technically, I'm the matron of honour because I'm an old married woman. Lucy's the bridesmaid, you're the best man and Tom's stepping in as a groomsman because Jake's cousin can't get away.'

'I see. Of course.'

It made sense. If Will had given any proper thought to the make-up of the wedding party, he should have known that Mattie would ask Lucy to be a bridesmaid. She was a vital member of their old 'gang'.

And he was totally cool about seeing her again, even though their relationship had been complicated since his brother's death eight years ago.

He was surprised, that was all, by the unexpected catch in his breath at the thought of seeing her again.

Lucy glanced in the rear-view mirror as her ute bounced down the rough country road towards town. *Cringe.* Her hair was limp and in dire need of a shampoo and she knew she looked decidedly scruffy.

She'd cleaned up carefully after delivering the calf, but she couldn't be sure that her hair and clothes were completely free of mud or straw. Steering one-handed, she tried to finger-comb loose strands into some kind of tidiness.

She wasn't wearing any make-up, and she was already in danger of arriving late for Mattie's wedding rehearsal, so she didn't have time to duck home for damage control. Not that it really mattered; tomorrow was the big day, after all. Not today.

But Will Carruthers would be at the rehearsal.

He was going to be best man at this wedding.

And why, after all this time, should that matter? Her crush on Will was ancient history. Water under the bridge. He was simply an old friend she'd almost lost touch with.

At least that was what she'd told herself for the past three months, ever since Mattie had announced her engagement and wedding plans. But, as she reached the outskirts of town, Lucy's body, to her annoyance, decided otherwise.

One glimpse of the little white church and the Carruthers family's elderly truck parked among the other vehicles on the green verge outside and Lucy's chest squeezed painfully. She felt as if she was breathing through cotton wool and her hands slipped on the steering wheel.

Her heart thumped.

Good grief, this was crazy. She'd known for twelve weeks now that Will would be a member of the wedding party. Why had she waited until the last moment to fall apart?

She parked the ute, dragged in a deep breath and closed her eyes, gave herself a stern lecture. She could do this. She was going to walk inside that little church with an easy stride and a smile on her face. She couldn't do much about her external appearance, but at least no one need guess she was a mess inside.

She would rather die than let on that she was jealous of Mattie for snaring and marrying a heart-throb like Jake. And she wouldn't turn the slightest hint of green when she cuddled Gina and Tom's darling babies.

More importantly, she would greet Will serenely.

She might even drop a light kiss on his cheek. After all, if her plans to marry Will's brother Josh hadn't been cruelly shattered, she would have been his sister-in-law.

OK.

She was only a few minutes late so she took a moment to check that her blouse was neatly tucked into her khaki jeans. Her boots were a bit dusty so she hastily wiped them with a tissue. There were no visible signs of the barn yard, thank heavens.

Feeling rather like a soldier going over the top of a trench, she didn't wait for second thoughts. She dived through the church doorway, cheery smile pinned in place, apologies for her lateness at the ready.

Thud. Will was standing at the end of the aisle, in front of the chancel steps, chatting to Jake.

Surreptitiously, Lucy devoured familiar details—the nut brown sheen of his hair, the outdoor glow on his skin and the creases at the corners of his eyes and mouth, his long legs in faded blue jeans.

As if these weren't enough to raise her temperature, she saw baby Mia, in a froth of pink, curled sleepily into the crook of Will's arm.

Heavens, had there ever been a sweeter place for a baby to sleep?

The tiny girl and the big man together made an image that she'd guiltily pictured in her most secret dreams and the sight of them now sucked vital air from her lungs.

Somehow she managed to walk down the aisle.

'Lucy!' Mattie called. 'I was just about to ring you.'

'I'm sorry I'm late. I was held up with a tricky calving.' She was surprised she could speak normally when her attention was riveted by Will, not just by how amazing he looked with that tiny pink bundle in his arms, but by the way his head swung abruptly at the sound of her voice and the way he went still and his eyes blazed suddenly.

Lucy felt as if the entire world had stopped, except for the frantic beating of her heart.

Thank heavens no one else seemed to notice.

'Don't worry,' Mattie was telling her calmly. 'We haven't been here long. I've just been going over the music with the organist.'

Everything was so suddenly normal and relaxed that Lucy was sure she'd misjudged Will's reaction. He certainly looked mega-cool and calm now as he greeted her. His light touch on her shoulder as he bent to kiss her and the merest brush of his lips on her cheek scalded her, but Will's grey eyes were perfectly calm.

He even looked mildly amused when he greeted her. 'Good to see you again, Lucy.'

In a matter of moments the babies were handed over to the minister's wife and daughter, who cooed and fussed over them in the front pew, while the members of the wedding party were taken through their paces.

Will, as the best man, would partner Gina. Lucy would process with Tom. So that was a relief. At least she didn't have to link arms and walk down the aisle with Will at the end of tomorrow's ceremony.

Lucy had been a bridesmaid twice before so she knew the ropes, but the minister wanted to explain every step of the service, and the rehearsal seemed to drag on and on.

On the plus side, she had time to calm down. This wedding was going to be a cinch. Nothing to get in a twist about.

Anyway, it was the height of self-indulgence to keep thinking about herself. Tomorrow was going to be Mattie's big day. Lucy, along with the entire population of Willowbank, loved warm-hearted, generous Mattie Carey and the whole township would probably turn out to watch her marry the hunky man of her dreams.

Lucy didn't want a single event or unhappy thought to mar this wedding's perfection.

Will who?

By the time the rehearsal was over, it was already dark outside, with a fragile fingernail moon hanging above the post office clock. The group dispersed quickly. Gina and Tom wanted to hurry home to get their babies settled. Mattie and Jake had to dash away to a special dinner Mattie's parents were hosting for assorted members of both families.

And Lucy wanted to hurry home to her 'boys', as she affectionately called her dogs. The Irish setter and the border collie enjoyed each other's company but, if she was away for any length of time, they were always frantic to see her.

She was fishing in her pocket for her car keys when she felt a tap on her elbow. She swung around to find herself trapped by Will Carruthers's smile, like a startled animal caught in a car's headlights.

'I haven't had a proper chance to say hello,' he said easily. 'I wanted to know how you are.'

Lucy gulped. 'I…I'm fine.' She was grateful that the darkness disguised the flush in her face, but it took a moment to remember to add, 'Thanks.' And, a frantic breath later, 'How about you, Will?'

'Not bad.' He gave her another smile and the skin around his eyes crinkled, then he shoved his hands into his jeans' pockets and stood in front of her with his long legs comfortably apart, shoulders wide. So tall and big he made her shiver.

She managed to ask, 'Are you still working in Mongolia?'

'Actually, no.' There was a slight pause and the tiniest

hint of an edgy chuckle. 'I was there long enough. Decided it's time for a change, so I'm going to look around for somewhere new.'

The news didn't surprise Lucy but, after so many years, she'd finally got used to Will's absence. When he was safely overseas she could almost forget about him. Almost.

Without quite meeting her gaze, Will said, 'Gina tells me you've bought a house.'

Lucy nodded. 'I bought the old Finnegan place at the end of Wicker Lane.' She shot him a rueful smile. 'It's a renovator's delight.'

'Sounds like a challenge.'

'A huge one.'

He lifted his gaze to meet hers and a glimmer of amusement lingered in his eyes. 'You were always one for a challenge.'

Lucy wasn't quite sure what Will meant by this. He might have been referring to the way she'd worked hard at her studies during their long ago friendship at university. Or it could have been a direct reference to the fact that she'd once been engaged to his chick-magnet older brother.

She tried to sound nonchalant. 'I haven't managed many renovations on the house yet. But at least there's plenty of room for my surgery and a nice big yard for the dogs.'

'How many dogs do you have now?'

She blinked with surprise at his unexpected question. 'Just the two still.'

'Seamus and Harry.'

'That's right.'

A small silence ticked by and Lucy felt awkward. She knew that if she'd met any other old friend from her school-days she would have offered an invitation to come back to her place. They could have shared a simple meal—probably pasta and a salad—eating in the kitchen, which she had at least partially renovated.

They could open a bottle of wine, catch up on old times, gossip about everything that had happened in the intervening years.

But her history with this man was too complicated. To start with, she'd never been able to completely snuff out the torch she carried for him, but that wasn't her only worry. Eight years ago, she'd made the terrible mistake of getting involved with his brother.

This was not the time, however, on the eve of Mattie and Jake's wedding, to rehash that sad episode.

From the darkness in the tree-lined creek behind the church a curlew's mournful cry drifted across the night and, almost as if it was a signal, Will took a step back. 'Well, I guess I'll see you tomorrow.'

'I dare say you won't be able to avoid it.'

Heavens, why had she said that? It sounded churlish. To make up for the gaffe, Lucy said quickly before he could leave, 'I'm so happy for Mattie. Jake seems like a really nice guy.'

'He's terrific,' Will agreed. 'And I'll have to hand it to Mattie. She succeeded in winning him when many others have failed.'

'Jake obviously adores her.'

'Oh, yeah, he's totally smitten.' Will looked suddenly uncomfortable and his shoulders lifted in an awkward shrug.

Lucy suspected this conversation was getting sticky for both of them.

'It's getting late,' she said gently. 'You'd better go. Your mother will have dinner waiting.'

He chuckled. 'That sounds like something from the dim dark ages when we were at high school.'

'Sorry,' she said, but he had already turned and was walking towards the truck.

He opened the squeaky door, then turned again and they both exchanged a brief wave before they climbed into their respective vehicles.

Lucy heard the elderly truck's motor rise in a harsh rev, then die down into a throaty lumbering growl. Will backed out of the parking spot and drove down the street and as she turned the key in her ute's ignition, she watched the truck's twin red tail lights growing smaller.

She remembered the times she'd driven with Will in that old truck of his father's, bumping over paddocks or down rough country lanes. Together they'd gone fossicking for sapphires, hunting for specks of gold down in the creek. At other times she'd urged him to help her to search for a new sub-species of fish.

They'd been great mates back then, but those days when Lucy had first moved to Willowbank with her dad after her parents' messy divorce felt like so very long ago now.

She had been sixteen and it was a horrible time, when she was angry with everyone. She'd been angry with her mother for falling in love with her boss, angry with her dad for somehow allowing it to happen, and angry with both of them for letting their marriage disintegrate in a heartbeat.

Most of all Lucy had been angry that she'd had to move away from Sydney to Willowbank. She'd hated leaving her old school and her friends to vegetate in a docile country town.

But then she'd met Will, along with Gina, Tom and Mattie and she'd soon been absorbed into a happy circle of friends who'd proved that life in the country could be every bit as good as life in the city.

OK, maybe her love of Willowbank had a lot to do with her feelings for Will, but at least she'd never let on how much she'd adored him. Instead, she'd waited patiently for him to realise that he loved her. When he took too long she'd taken matters into her own hands and it had all gone horribly wrong.

But it was so, so unhelpful to be thinking about that now.

Even so, Lucy was fighting tears as she reversed the ute. And, as she drove out of town, she was bombarded by bittersweet, lonely memories.

CHAPTER TWO

THE impact of the explosion sent Will flying, tossed him like a child's rag toy and dumped him hard. He woke with his heart thudding, his nerves screaming as he gripped at the bed sheets.

Bed sheets?

At first he couldn't think how he'd arrived back in the bedroom of his schooldays, but then he slowly made sense of his surroundings.

He was no longer in Mongolia.

He was safe.

He wished it had all been a nightmare, but it was unfortunately true. He'd been conducting a prospecting inspection of an old abandoned mine when it had blown without warning. By some kind of miracle he'd escaped serious injury, but his two good friends were dead.

That was the savage reality. He'd been to the funerals of both Barney and Keith—one in Brisbane and the other in Ottawa.

He'd been to hell and back sitting in those separate chapels, listening to heartbreaking eulogies and wondering why he'd been spared when his friends had so not deserved to die.

And yet here he was, home at Tambaroora…

Where nothing had changed…

Squinting in the shuttered moonlight, Will could see the bookshelf that still held his old school textbooks. His swimming trophies lined the shelf above the bed, and he knew without looking that the first geological specimens he'd collected were in a small glass case on the desk beneath the window.

Even the photo of him with his brother, Josh, was still there on the dresser. It showed Will squashed onto a pathetic little tricycle that he was clearly too big for, while Josh looked tall and grown-up on his first two-wheeler bike.

Will rolled over so he couldn't see the image. He didn't want to be reminded that his brother had beaten him to just about everything that was important in his life. It hadn't been enough for Josh Carruthers to monopolise their father's affection, he'd laid first claim on Tambaroora and he'd won the heart of Will's best friend.

That might have been OK if Josh had taken good care of Lucy.

An involuntary sigh whispered from Will's lips.

Lucy.

Seeing her again tonight had unsettled him on all kinds of levels.

When he closed his eyes he could see the silvery-white gleam of moonlight on her hair as they'd stood outside the church. He could hear the familiar soft lilt in her voice.

Damn it. He'd wanted to tell her about the accident. He needed to talk about it.

He hadn't told his family because he knew it would upset his mother. Jessie Carruthers had already lost one son and she didn't need the news of her surviving son's brush with death.

Will could have talked to Jake, of course. They'd worked together in Mongolia and Jake would have understood how upset he was, but he hadn't wanted to throw a wet blanket on the eve of his mate's wedding.

No, Lucy was the one person he would have liked to talk to. In the past, they'd often talked long into the night. As students they'd loved deep and meaningful discussions.

Yes, he could have told Lucy what he'd learned at those funerals.

But it was probably foolish to think he could resurrect the closeness they'd enjoyed as students.

After all this time, they'd both changed.

Hell, was it really eight years? He could still feel the shock of that December day when he'd been skiing in Norway and he'd received the news that Lucy and his brother were engaged to be married. He'd jumped on the first plane home.

With a groan, Will flung aside the sheet and swung out of bed, desperate to throw off the memories and the sickening guilt and anger that always accompanied his thoughts of that terrible summer.

But, with the benefit of hindsight, Will knew he'd been unreasonably angry with Josh for moving in on his best friend while his back was turned. He'd had no claim on Lucy. She'd never been his girlfriend. He'd gone overseas with Cara Howard and, although their relationship hadn't lasted, he'd allowed himself to be distracted by new sights, new people, new adventures.

He'd let life take him by the hand, happy to go with the flow, finding it easier than settling down.

The news that Josh was going to marry Lucy shouldn't have upset him, but perhaps he might have coped more easily if Lucy had chosen to marry a stranger. As it was, he'd never been able to shake off the feeling that Josh had moved in on her just to prove to his little brother that he could have whatever he desired.

Unfortunately, Will had chosen the very worst time to have it out with Josh.

He would never, to the end of his days, forget the early morning argument at the airfield, or Josh's stubbornness, or the sight of that tiny plane tumbling out of the sky like an autumn leaf.

If only that had been the worst of it, but it was Gina who'd told him that the shock of Josh's death had caused Lucy to have a miscarriage.

A miscarriage?

Will had been plagued by endless questions—questions he'd had no right to ask. Which had come first—the engagement or the pregnancy? Had Josh truly loved Lucy?

A week after the funeral he'd tried to speak to her, but Dr McKenty had been fiercely protective of his daughter and he'd turned Will away.

So the only certainties that he'd been left with were Josh's death and Lucy's loss, and he'd found it pitifully easy to take the blame for both.

To make amends, he'd actually tried to stay on at Tambaroora after Josh's death. But he couldn't replace Josh in his father's eyes and he'd soon known that he didn't fit in any more. He was a piece from a flashy foreign jigsaw trying to fit into a homemade puzzle.

For Will, it had made sense to leave again and to stay away longer. In time, he'd trained himself to stop dwelling on the worst of it. But of course he couldn't stay away from his home and family for ever and there were always going to be times, like now, when everything came back to haunt him.

* * *

Lucy dreamed about Will.

In her dream they were back at Sydney University and they'd met in the refectory for coffee and to compare notes after a chemistry practical.

It was an incredibly simple but companionable scene. She and Will had always enjoyed hanging out together, and in her dream they were sitting at one of the little tables overlooking the courtyard, chatting and smiling and discussing the results of their latest experiments.

When it was time to leave for separate lectures, Lucy announced calmly, as if it was a normal extension of their everyday conversation, 'Oh, by the way, Will, I'm pregnant.'

Will's face broke into a beautiful smile and he drew her into his arms and hugged her, and Lucy knew that her pregnancy was the perfect and natural expression of their love.

She felt the special protection of his arms about her and she was filled with a sense of perfect happiness, of well-being, of everything being right in her world.

When she woke, she lay very still with her eyes closed, lingering for as long as she could in the happy afterglow of the dream, clinging to the impossible fantasy that she was pregnant.

Better than that, she was pregnant with Will's baby. Not his brother's…

The dream began to fade and she could no longer ignore the fact that morning sunlight was pulsing on the other side of her closed eyelids.

Reality reared its unwelcome head.

Damn.

Not that dream again. How stupid.

Actually, it was more like a recurring nightmare, so far divorced from Lucy's real life that she always felt sick when she woke. She hated to think that her subconscious could still, after all this time, play such cruel tricks on her.

In truth, she'd never been brave enough to let her friendship with Will progress into anything deeper. At university, she'd seen all the other girls who'd fallen for him. She'd watched Will date them for a while and then move on, and she'd decided it was safer to simply be his buddy. His friend.

As his girlfriend she'd risk losing him and she couldn't have coped with that. If they remained good friends, she could keep him for ever.

Or so she'd thought.

The plan had serious flaws, of course, which was no doubt why she was still plagued far too often by the dream.

But now, as Lucy opened her eyes, she knew it was time to wake up to more important realities. This wasn't just any morning. It was Mattie's wedding day.

This was a day for hair appointments and manicures, helping Mattie to dress and smiling for photographs. This was to be her friend's perfect day.

Get over it, Lucy.

Get over yourself.

Stifling a lingering twinge of longing for the dream, she threw off the bedclothes, went to the window and looked out. It was a beautiful day, cloudless and filled with sunshine. She smiled.

No more useless longings. No more doleful thoughts.

Surely clear blue skies were a very promising omen?

In Willowbank everyone was abuzz.

With the help of friends and relatives from around the

district, Mattie's mum had grown masses of white petunias in pots and tubs and even in wheelbarrows.

Lucy happily helped a team of women to unload containers of flowers from their cars and place them strategically in the church and the grounds, as well as the marquee where the reception was to be held in an allotment next to the church hall. The instant floral effect was spectacular.

After that, the morning passed in a happy whirl, much to Lucy's relief. First, she met up with Mattie and Gina at the hairdresser's, then they popped into the salon next door for matching manicures, and finally they dashed back to Mattie's for a delicious light lunch prepared by one of her doting aunts.

During lunch the phone seemed never to stop ringing and all kinds of messages flew back and forth. Gina's mum, who was babysitting the twins, reported that they'd been fed and burped and were sleeping beautifully. Nurses from the Sydney hospital where the babies had been born rang to wish Mattie and Jake all the best for married life. The caterer had a question about the positioning of the wedding cake on the main table.

Lucy had to admire the way Mattie seemed to float through it all. She was the most serene bride ever. Nothing bothered her or was too much trouble. Mattie had always been sweet and easy-going, but she'd never been as blissfully relaxed and happy and confident as she was today.

It must be love, Lucy thought, and she wished it was contagious.

Shortly after lunch, the excitement really began. Refrigerated boxes arrived from the florist, filled with truly gorgeous bouquets. Then it was time for the girls to put on their make-up, laughing as they took turns in front of

Mattie's bedroom mirror, the same mirror where years ago they had first experimented with mascara and eyeliner while they'd gossiped about boys.

Back then, Lucy, being older and from the city, had been considered to be wiser and worldlier. The other girls had looked up to her with undisguised respect and considerable awe.

How the tables had turned. Now Gina was married and a mother, and Mattie was about to marry Jake, while Lucy was…

No! She wasn't going to tolerate a single negative thought today.

When they'd achieved their best with make-up, Gina and Lucy slipped into their bridesmaid's dresses, which were simply divine. The palest pink duchess satin looked equally pretty on Gina with her dark hair and olive complexion as it did on Lucy, who was blonde and fair-skinned.

Then it was time to fuss over Mattie, to fasten the dozens of tiny satin-covered buttons down her back, to help to secure her veil and then to gasp in sheer astonishment when they saw the completed picture of their best friend in her wedding gown.

'You look absolutely breathtaking,' Lucy whispered.

Gina was emotional. 'You're so beautiful Jake's going to cry when he sees you.'

'Please don't say that.' Mattie laughed nervously. 'You'll make *me* cry.'

'And me,' moaned Lucy.

Already, at the mere thought of an emotional bridegroom, she could feel mascara-threatening tears about to spill.

Oh, help. Weddings were such poignant affairs. And

today Will was going to be there, looking dashing as the best man. How on earth was she going to get through the next few hours?

Dressed in matching dark formal suits with silver ties and orange blossoms in their lapels, Jake, Will and Tom were ushered into the minuscule vestry and instructed to wait till it was time to take their places at the front of the church.

Will anxiously patted a pocket in his suit jacket. 'The rings are still safe.'

Jake grinned and laid a reassuring hand on his friend's shoulder. 'That's the third time you've checked the rings in the past five minutes. Relax, man, they're not going to grow legs and run away.'

'Jake's the guy who's supposed to be nervous,' added Tom with a grin.

Will nodded and tried to smile. 'Sorry. Don't know what's got into me.' He shot Jake a questioning glance. 'Aren't you even a little nervous?'

'Why should I be nervous?'

'You're getting married.' Will wished his voice wasn't so hoarse. His sleepless night was really getting to him. 'It's par for the course for a bridegroom to have the jitters,' he said.

'But I'm marrying Mattie,' Jake responded simply, as if that explained everything. And his glowing smile made it patently clear that he knew, without doubt, he was the luckiest man alive.

Will wished he felt a fraction of his mate's happiness.

'So where are you heading for your honeymoon?' he asked. 'Or is that a state secret?'

Jake grinned. 'The exact location is a surprise for

Mattie, but I'll tell you two.' He lowered his voice. 'I'm taking her to Italy. She's never been overseas, so we're going to Venice, Lake Como and the Amalfi Coast.'

'Wow!' Tom's jaw dropped. 'That's so over the top it's fabulous. You'll have an amazing time.'

Jake nodded happily but, before he could say anything else, the minister appeared at the vestry door and sent them a smiling wink. 'Could you come this way now please, gentlemen?'

A chill ran down Will's spine. For crying out loud, what was the matter with him today? Anyone would think he was the one getting married, or that they were criminals being led to the dock.

'All the best, mate,' he whispered gruffly to Jake.

'Thanks.'

The two friends shook hands, then headed through the little doorway that led into the church, where an incredible transformation had occurred.

Not only was the place packed to the rafters with people dressed in their best finery, but there were flowers and white ribbons everywhere—dangling from the ends of pews, wound around columns, adorning windowsills and filling vases, large and small.

And there was organ music, billowing and rippling like the background music in a sentimental movie. Will tried to swallow the lump in his throat. Why was it that weddings were designed to zero straight in on unsuspecting emotions?

He glanced at Jake and saw his Adam's apple jerk.

'You OK?' he whispered out of the side of his mouth.

'I'll be fine once Mattie gets here.'

'She won't be late,' Will reassured him and again he nervously patted the rings in his pocket.

There was a flurry in the little porch at the back of the church and, as if everyone had been choreographed, the congregation turned. Will felt fine hairs lift on the back of his neck. His stomach tightened.

The girls appeared in a misty mirage of white and pink. Will blinked. Lucy, Gina and Mattie looked incredibly out-of-this-world beautiful in long feminine dresses and glamorous hairstyles, and with their arms filled with flowers.

He heard Jake catch his breath, felt goosebumps lift on his arms.

The organist struck a dramatic chord.

Lucy and Gina, apparently satisfied with their arrangement of Mattie's dress and veil, took their places in front of her, Lucy first.

Will couldn't be sure that he wasn't trembling.

Lucy stood, shoulders back, looking straight ahead, with her blonde head high, her blue eyes smiling. To Will she looked vulnerable and yet resolute and his heart began to thunder loudly.

It was so weird.

He'd seen countless weddings and endless processions of bridesmaids, but none of them had made him feel the way he felt now as the organist began to play and Lucy began to walk down the aisle with her smile carefully in place.

She'd always tried to pretend she was a tomboy, keeping her hair short and wispy and preferring to live in T-shirts and jeans, but today nothing could hide her femininity.

Her pastel off-the-shoulders dress and the soft pink lilies in her arms highlighted the paleness of her hair, the honey-gold tints in her skin, the pink lushness of her lips. She had never looked lovelier.

Except perhaps…that one night on a shadowy veranda, when she'd turned to him with tears in her eyes…

He willed her to look at him. Just one glance would do. For old friendship's sake. He wanted eye contact, needed to send her one smile, longed for one tiny link with her.

Come on, look this way, Lucy.

She smiled at the people in the congregation, at her particular friends, at Jake, but her gaze didn't flicker any further to the right. It was clear she did not want to see Will.

Or, perhaps, she simply felt no need.

CHAPTER THREE

LUCY'S eyes were distinctly misty as she watched Mattie and Jake dance the bridal waltz. They looked so happy together and so deeply in love. She was sure everyone watching them felt misty-eyed too.

It had been an utterly perfect wedding.

The beautiful ceremony had been followed by a happy procession across Willowbank's main street to the marquee where the reception was held. Champagne flowed, a string quartet played glorious music and the guests were served delectable food.

Jake's speech had been heartfelt and touching and Will's toast was appropriately witty, although he went embarrassingly over the top with his praise for the bridesmaids. Lucy had felt her face flame when curious eyes had swung in her direction and the cutting of the cake had been a welcome distraction.

Everyone had broken into spontaneous cheering for Mattie and Jake, and Lucy was thrilled. The wedding couldn't have been happier.

She was relieved that she'd survived without making a fool of herself. Which mostly meant avoiding Will—a tall order given that her eyes had developed a habit of sneaking in his direction whenever she thought he wasn't looking. She'd tried so hard to ignore him, but she'd always thought he was the best-looking guy ever.

She could still remember the day she'd first met him as a schoolboy down by Willow Creek, crouched at the edge of the water.

Even viewing him from behind, he'd been beautiful.

He'd taken his shirt off and he'd been squatting, reaching down, panning for gold in the water. Sunlight breaking through overhead trees had lent an extra sheen to his dark brown hair and to the smooth golden-brown skin on his back.

Lucy hadn't been able to help staring. His shoulders were wide, his hips narrow, his limbs long—the build of a swimmer.

Now, so many years later, he was even more irresistible in his dark formal attire. Lucy kept finding things she needed to check out—the manly jut of his jaw above the crisp collar, the neat line of his dark hair across the back of his neck, the stunning breadth of his shoulders in the stylish suit jacket…

Sigh…

Despite the wedding's perfection, the evening had been a huge strain and she was worn out.

She'd kicked off her high heeled shoes and they were now stowed under the table. She was thinking rather fondly about the end of the night when she could head for home. It would be so nice to greet her dogs, then curl up in bed with a glass of water and a headache tablet.

Tom leaned towards her. 'Lucy, it's our turn to dance.'

She winced. 'Is it really?'

Tom was already on his feet. 'Come on. Gina and Will are already up. You know the wedding party is expected to take a twirl on the dance floor.'

Bother. She'd forgotten about that. She suppressed a sigh as she fished beneath the table for her shoes. *Ouch.* They pinched as she squeezed back into them.

She looked over at the dance floor and saw that Tom was right. Gina was already dancing with Will and, for no reason that made sense, her silly heart began to trip and stumble.

'Lead the way,' she told Tom resolutely, slipping her arm through his. Thank heavens he was a reliable old friend. At least she could dance with Tom till the cows came home without being attacked by dangerous palpitations.

Unfortunately, Tom didn't seem to be quite so enamoured with her as his dancing partner. At the end of the bracket, other couples joined them on the dance floor and Tom leaned close to her ear. 'Would you mind if I asked Gina for a dance?'

'Of course I don't mind.' She took a step back to prove it. 'Please, go ahead. You must dance with your wife.'

Tom happily tapped Will on the back and Lucy retreated to the edge of the timber dance floor. Over her shoulder, she watched the men's brief smiling exchange. She saw Will's nod and her heart began to race as she guessed what might happen next.

It was logical—a common courtesy for Will to ask *her* to dance—but there were times when logic and courtesy flew out of the window. Times like now, when her out of date, unhelpful feelings for Will made simple things complicated.

On the surface, one quick dance with an old friend should have been a piece of cake. But on a super-romantic night like tonight, Lucy was trembling at the very thought of dancing publicly in Will Carruthers's arms.

She couldn't help thinking about that kiss all those years ago, when she'd made a fool of herself at Will's farewell party. She turned, planning to hurry back to her place at the table.

'Lucy!'

Will's voice sounded close behind her and she froze.

'I won't let you escape that easily.' His tone held a thread of humour, but there was also a note of command that was hard to ignore.

His hand brushed her wrist and the touch was like a fire-brand. Lucy was helpless as his fingers enclosed around her, as he pulled her gently but decisively towards him. 'Come on,' he urged. 'We've got to have one dance.'

He made it sound easy, but when she looked into his cool grey eyes she was surprised to see a cautious edge to his smile, as if he wasn't quite as confident as he sounded. Which didn't help her to relax.

A number of wedding guests were watching them, however, and the last thing she wanted was a scene.

'One dance?' Lucy forced lightness into her voice. 'Why not?' She managed a smile. No way did she want to give the impression she was trying to dodge Will. One dance was no problem at all. She would dance with him till her feet fell off.

Will led her back onto the dance floor.

Gulp.

As soon as he placed one hand at her back and took her other hand in his, she knew this wasn't going to be any version of easy. She drew a jagged breath.

'Smile,' Will murmured as he pulled her closer. 'This is a wedding, not a funeral.'

He took the lead and Lucy obediently pinned on a smile. She'd only danced with Will a handful of times, long ago. Even so, she could remember every single detail—his habit of enfolding her fingers inside his, the way he smelled of midnight, and the way her head was exactly level with his jaw.

Tonight, every familiar memory felt like a pulled thread, unravelling her poorly stitched self control. Being this close to Will played havoc with her heartbeats, with her sense of rhythm. She kept stumbling and bumping into him and then apologising profusely.

After the third apology, he steered her to the edge of the floor and he leaned back a little, and he smiled as he looked into her face.

Will said something, but Lucy couldn't hear him above the music and she shook her head, lifted her shoulders to show she had no idea.

Leaning closer, she felt her skin vibrate as he spoke into her ear. 'Are you OK? Would you like a break?'

That would be sensible, wouldn't it?

She nodded. 'Yes, please.'

A reprieve.

Maybe not. Will stayed close beside her as she returned to the table and, before she could resume her seat, he said, 'There are chairs outside. Why don't we go out there where it's cooler and quieter, away from the music?'

Lucy's heart stumbled again. Going outside where it was quieter suggested that Will wanted to talk.

Part of her yearned to talk with him, but she wasn't sure it was wise. What could they talk about now? They'd covered the basics last night after the rehearsal, and Will had been away for so long that they'd lost their old sense of camaraderie.

Besides, further conversation would surely lead to uncomfortable topics like her relationship with Josh. Wouldn't it be wiser to simply keep their distance now?

But the look in Will's eyes as he watched her sent a fine shiver rushing over her skin and she knew that wisdom would lose this particular battle and curiosity would win. She secretly longed to hear what Will wanted to talk about.

'I'm sure a little fresh air is a good idea,' she said and she went with him through a doorway in the side of the marquee into the moon silvered night.

They found two chairs abandoned by smokers and, as soon as Lucy sat down, she slipped off her shoes and rubbed at her aching feet.

Will chuckled softly.

'I'm not used to wearing such high heels,' she said defensively. 'You should try them. They're sheer torture.'

'I don't doubt that for a moment, but they look sensational.' He released a button on his jacket, letting it fall open. His shirt gleamed whitely in the moonlight and he stretched his long legs in front of him.

After a small pause, he said, 'I meant what I said in my speech. You look lovely tonight, Lucy.'

Her cheeks grew warm again. 'Thanks. Mattie chose our dresses. She has very feminine tastes.'

He let her self-effacing comment pass.

'It's been a perfect wedding,' she said to make amends, but then she was ambushed by an involuntary yawn. 'But it seems to have worn me out.'

'You've probably been working too hard.'

She shook her head. 'My work doesn't very often make me tired. Weddings, on the other hand…'

'Can be very draining.'

'Yes.'

He was watching her with a lopsided smile. 'It's not always easy to watch your friends tie the knot.'

'I…' Her mouth was suddenly dry and her tongue stuck to its roof. She shot Will a sharp glance, uncertain where this conversation was heading. She tried again. 'I'm really happy for Mattie, aren't you?'

'Absolutely,' he said. 'Marriage couldn't have happened to a nicer girl.'

Lucy nodded. A small silence limped by. 'I suppose weddings are tiring because they involve lots of people.' Hunting for a way to disguise the fact that Will's presence at this wedding was her major problem, she made a sweeping gesture towards the crowded marquee. 'I'm more used to animals these days. They're so much quieter than humans.'

'And I'm used to rocks.'

Lucy laughed. 'I dare say they're quieter too.'

'Silence is one of their better attributes.' Will chuckled again. 'Sounds like we've turned into a pair of old loners.'

'Maybe,' she said softly, but she knew it was hazardous for her to talk of such things with this man.

Quietly, he said, 'It's happening all around us, Goose.'

Goose…her old nickname.

Only her father and Will had ever called her Goose, or Lucy Goose…and hearing the name now made her dangerously nostalgic.

She tried to shake that feeling aside. 'What's happening all around us?'

'Friends getting married. Starting families.'

Lucy stiffened. Why did he have to bring up *that* subject? 'It's hardly surprising, given our friends' ages.'

'Yes, and we're older than all of them.'

Tick tock, tick tock, tick tock…

Lucy closed her eyes as the familiar breathless panic

gripped her. *No.* She wasn't going to think about *that* worry tonight. She'd declared a moratorium on all thoughts that involved babies, having babies, wanting babies, losing babies. She couldn't imagine why Will had raised such a sensitive topic.

Or perhaps he didn't know about her miscarriage. After his brother's death, she'd barely spoken to Will at the funeral and then he'd moved as far away from Willowbank as was humanly possible. Since then, if they'd run into each other, it had been by accident, or because their friends had invited them to the same Christmas party.

Will had always been polite but he'd kept his distance and Lucy had always been busily proving to him that she was managing damn fine splendid on her own.

So why this?

Why now?

Lucy knew her sudden breathless fear would not be helped by a continued discussion of marriage and babies with Will Carruthers.

'Is there a point to this conversation, Will?' She thrust her feet back into her shoes and grimaced as they pinched. 'Because I don't enjoy being reminded of how old I'm getting.'

She jumped to her feet, only to discover she was shaking violently. Her knees had no strength whatsoever and she had no choice but to sink down again.

She was too embarrassed to look at Will.

In a heartbeat, he was bending over her solicitously. 'I'm sorry. I thought I was stating the obvious. Marriages, births, christenings all around us. Are you all right? Can I get you a drink?'

'I'm fine,' she lied, dragging in oxygen. 'But I…I should go back inside. Mattie might need me.'

'Are you sure you're OK?'

She gulped another deep breath. 'I'm certain.'

Will's hand was at her elbow, supporting her as she got to her feet again, and she hoped he couldn't feel the way her body trembled.

With her first step she swayed against him. He put his arm around her and it felt amazingly fabulous to have his solid shoulder to lean on. 'I swear I haven't had too much to drink,' she said.

'I know that. You're just tired.'

She supposed he was right. What else could it be?

'As soon as this reception is over, I'll drive you home,' Will said.

'There's no need.'

'No arguments, Lucy. You don't have your car here, do you?'

'No,' she admitted. 'I left it at Mattie's place.'

'My vehicle's here. If you're tired, you need a lift.'

By now they'd reached the doorway to the marquee and Lucy could see Gina handing around a platter of wedding cake in pink and silver parcels.

'Oh, heavens,' she cried, slipping from Will's hold. 'I should be helping with the cake.'

'Are you sure you're up to it?'

'Of course.'

And, as she hurried to help, she knew that it was true. She was perfectly fine when she was safely away from Will.

That went well, Will thought wryly as he watched Lucy hand around platters of wedding cake.

Already she was smiling and chatting and looking a hundred times happier than she had a few minutes ago when he'd crassly reminded her that life was passing them by.

Watching her with a thoughtful frown, he recalled the countless conversations they'd enjoyed when they were friends. They'd shared a mutual interest in science, and so they'd been totally in tune about many things. It was only later, when they'd talked about life after university, that their friendship had run into trouble.

Lucy was adventurous and as curious about the world as he was, but unlike him, she hadn't been keen to get away. She'd apparently wanted nothing more than to get straight back to Willowbank, to settle down in a veterinary practice.

Her father was a doctor and she'd claimed that she was anxious to follow his example. She'd worked hard to get her degree and she looked on travel as a waste of time. Why work at menial jobs simply to earn enough money to move on to the next travel spot, when she could stay in Willowbank and build her career?

At the time, when Will had left on his big adventure with Cara in tow, he'd had a vague idea that he might eventually return and find work closer to home.

The news of his brother's engagement to Lucy McKenty had come out of the blue and he'd been shocked by how much it had worried him, by the urge that had hit him to hurry home. Not that he could blame Lucy for falling in love with Josh.

Everyone in the entire Willow Creek district had loved his outgoing, confident brother—and Josh Carruthers had a habit of getting what he wanted, especially when it came to women.

Will could easily imagine how his brother had flirted with Lucy. Hell, yeah. Josh would have charmed and courted her so expertly she wouldn't have known what had hit her. And Josh would have offered her the exact life she wanted—marriage and a family, with a sheep station thrown in as the icing on the cake.

But had Josh really, deeply cared for Lucy? Had he wanted to make her happy?

It surprised Will that he still let these questions bother him after all this time.

'You look down in the mouth.' Jake's voice sounded at Will's elbow. 'Everything OK?'

Will turned guiltily and forced a grin. 'It's been a fabulous night,' he said, hoping to avoid answering Jake's question. 'Ace wedding, mate.'

'Glad you've had a good time.' Jake nodded his head in Lucy's direction. 'She's a lovely girl.'

It was pointless to pretend he didn't know who Jake meant. Will nodded. 'Yeah.' He shoved his hands deep in his pockets, as if the action could somehow comfort him.

'Mattie told me you two used to be really close.'

'Close friends,' Will corrected and he did his best to dismiss this with a shrug, but Jake was watching him in a way that made his neck burn hotly.

Jake smiled. 'You look as miserable as I felt four months ago, before I sorted everything out with Mattie.'

'This is totally different. More like a mystery than history,' Will muttered glumly.

'Perhaps. But, in the end, it all comes down to the same thing.'

Will glared at his friend. 'I didn't realise that a marriage ceremony turned a man into an instant relationship guru.'

Jake's smile faded. 'Sorry. Was I sounding smug?'

'You were.' Will gave another shrug. 'But I'd probably be smug too, if I was in your shoes.'

'Except that you're right,' Jake said, looking more serious now. 'I know nothing about you and Lucy.'

A heavy sigh escaped Will and he realised that, despite his fierce reaction, he'd actually been hoping that his friend could reveal some kind of magic insight that would help him to clear the air with Lucy. Anything to be rid of this gnawing guilt he still carried.

'I think we're heading off soon,' Jake said. 'I guess I'd better find my wife and finish our farewells.'

They shook hands and Will wished his mate all the best and it wasn't much later before the guests started gathering on the footpath to wave the happy couple off.

In the light of a street lamp, Will could see Lucy's golden hair shimmering palely as she kissed Mattie and Jake, before she drifted back to watch their departure from the edge of the crowd.

Mattie was laughing as she stood at the car's open door and lifted her bouquet of white roses. Will saw Lucy backing even further away, almost trying to hide.

Then the roses were sailing through the air in a high arc. There were girlish squeals of laughter and hands rose to try to grab the flowers, but Mattie's aim was sure. The bouquet landed square on Lucy's nose and she had no choice but to catch it.

A cheer went up and Lucy gave a bashful smile and held the bouquet high, no doubt knowing that all of Willowbank would love to see their favourite vet married.

But she was probably grateful that everyone's attention quickly returned to the bride and groom. Jake was already helping Mattie into the car.

Over the heads of the crowd he sent Will a flashing grin and Will answered with a thumbs-up.

The car's exhaust roared as they took off and the rear window was covered in 'just married' signs written in toothpaste, which only served to prove how old-fashioned this town really was.

Will, however, was watching Lucy. She stood in the shadows at the back of the throng, clutching the wedding bouquet in one hand while she used the other hand to swipe at her tears.

CHAPTER FOUR

LUCY wished the ground would open up and swallow her. It was bad enough that everyone knew the bride had deliberately thrown the bouquet to her. To cry about it was beyond pathetic, but to do so in front of Will Carruthers was more embarrassing than she could bear.

Turning her back on him, she gave one final swipe and an unladylike sniff and she willed her eyes to stay dry. It wasn't a moment too soon.

Will's voice sounded close behind her. 'We can leave whenever you like,' he said.

She drew a deep slow breath and turned to him with a smile on her face. Any number of people would have given her a lift, but she was determined to show Will that his comments about the two of them being a pair of old loners had not upset her.

'Could you give me just a moment?' she said. 'I'd like to say goodbye to a few people.'

'By all means. I've said my farewells. Let me know when you're ready.'

'I shouldn't be long, unless Mrs Carey needs my help with anything else. Shall I meet you at the truck?'

'Sure.'

It was crazy the way her stomach tightened as she crossed the road to Will's parked truck. Crazier still the way her heart thrashed when she saw his tall figure waiting in the shadows beside the vehicle. He stepped forward when he saw her and the white shirt beneath his jacket glowed in the moonlight. Fire flashed in his light grey eyes.

'Let me help you up,' he said as he opened the truck's passenger door.

'I can manage.' Lucy was anxious to avoid his gallantry. If Will touched her now, she might self-combust.

But managing alone wasn't easy. With her arms filled with her bridesmaid's bouquet as well as the bride's white roses and with the added complication of her long straight skirt and precarious high heels, the whole business of clambering up into the truck was fraught with difficulties.

Will was full of apologies. 'I forgot how hard it is to climb into this damned thing.'

'If you hold the bouquets, I'm sure I can swing myself up.'

Without waiting for his reply, Lucy thrust the flowers into his arms. Then, grateful for the darkness, she yanked her skirt with one hand and took a firm grip of the door handle with the other. She stepped high and hauled herself up, and everything would have been fine if one of her high heels hadn't caught on the step.

In mid-flight she lost her balance and then lost her grip on the handle and, before she could recover, she was slipping backwards.

Into Will's arms.

She was crushed against his chest, along with several dozen blooms.

'I've got you.'

Lucy wasn't sure if the pounding of Will's heart and his

sharp intake of breath were caused by shock or the exertion of catching her.

Desperately, she tried to ignore how wonderfully safe she felt in his arms, how beyond fabulous it was to be cradled against his splendidly muscular chest. The wool of his expensive suit was cool and fine beneath her cheek. She could have stayed there…

'I'm sorry,' she spluttered. 'Anyone would think I was drunk.'

'The thought never crossed my mind.'

'You can put me down, Will. I'm quite all right.'

'I think it might be better if we do this my way.'

His face was in darkness so Lucy couldn't see his expression, but his voice was deep and warm, like a comforting blanket around her, and he hoisted her up onto the front seat of the truck with astonishing ease.

'Put your seat belt on,' he said, as if she was a child. 'And then I'll pass you what's left of the bouquets.'

Chastened, Lucy thanked him.

The glorious scent of crushed rose petals filled the truck's cabin as Will climbed behind the wheel and pulled the driver's door shut. But the fragrance couldn't disguise the smell of ancient leather and it couldn't block Lucy's memories.

This was the first time in ten years that she'd been alone in the dark with Will, and stupidly she remembered that embarrassing kiss on the shadowy veranda at Tambaroora. She could remember exactly how he'd tasted and the warm pressure of his lips, the sexy slide of his tongue….

He turned to her. 'Are you OK now?'

'Perfectly,' she said in a choked whisper.

'Are you sure?' he asked, frowning at her, watching her intently.

She pressed a hand against her heart in a bid to calm its wicked thudding. 'I was hobbled by this jolly dress and I slipped in the stupid heels.' She sounded more astringent than she'd meant to. 'After tonight, these shoes are going straight to the Country Women's second-hand store.'

Will chuckled softly, then started the truck and soon they were rumbling down the street. Lucy buried her nose in the roses, glad that he didn't try to talk all the way home.

But, in the silence, her thoughts turned back to their earlier conversation. Will had shocked her when he'd raised the subject of marriage and babies, but perhaps she shouldn't have been so surprised. It was, as he'd said, happening all around them. Gina and Tom had their twins. Mattie was married.

She had been so busy trying to back away from the topic, so scared Will would discover how hung up she was about these very things, that she'd cut the conversation short.

Now she was left to wonder. Had he actually been leading up to something he wanted to discuss? She'd always been hurt by Will's silence after Josh's death and the miscarriage. He'd never given her the chance to confess why she'd become involved with his brother.

Of course, it would be dreadfully difficult to tell him the truth, but she'd always felt guilty and she wanted to come clean. Perhaps then she would be able to put it behind her at last. She might, at last, stop dreaming about Will.

As the truck rumbled down country lanes, past darkened farmhouses and quiet paddocks, a number of questions bumped around in her head and by the time Will pulled up in front of her house, Lucy couldn't hold back. 'Will, what was the point you wanted to make?'

In the glow of the dashboard's lights, she could see his frown. 'I'm sorry, Lucy, you've lost me.'

'When we were talking at the wedding, you were carrying on about how old we are now and I got in a huff, but were you actually trying to make a point?'

He turned to face her, one hand draped loosely over the steering wheel. 'Nothing in particular.' He smiled shyly. 'I simply wanted to talk to you—the way we used to.'

A ghost of a smile trickled across his face. Then he looked out through the windscreen and tapped his fingers on the steering wheel. 'We have a lot to catch up on, but it's late. Why don't I give you a call some time?'

How could such a simple question send her insides into turmoil? It was so silly to be incredibly excited simply because Will Carruthers planned to talk to her again.

With difficulty, Lucy overcame her desperate curiosity to know what he wanted to talk about. She managed to speak calmly.

'I'll wait to hear from you, then,' she said as she pushed the door open.

'Don't move,' Will ordered, shoving his door open too. 'I'll help you out. I don't want you falling again. You're an accident waiting to happen tonight.'

A hasty glance at the huge step down to the road showed Lucy the wisdom of accepting his offer, but her heart skipped several beats as he rounded the truck and helped her down.

'Thank you,' she said demurely. 'My elderly bones couldn't have taken another stumble this evening.'

His soft laugh held the hint of a growl. 'Get to bed, Grandma.'

To her astonishment, Will's lips feathered the merest brush of a kiss against her temple. Her knees almost gave way.

'Perhaps I should escort you to the door,' he said.

'I think I'm still capable of tottering up my own front path.'

'I'll wait here till you're safely inside.'

After years of being fiercely independent, Lucy had to admit it was rather pleasant to have a lordly male watching out for her. With the bouquets bundled in one arm, she lifted her skirt elegantly and took careful dainty steps as she made her way up the uneven brick path.

She'd left her car and her other set of keys at Mattie's parents' house, but there was a spare key under the flowerpot on the porch. Tonight, however, there was more than a flowerpot on the porch. A hessian bag had been left on the doorstep.

Lucy saw it and sighed. Caring for wildlife wasn't part of her veterinary responsibilities, but people knew she had a soft heart and they were always bringing her injured bush creatures. Animals hit by cars were the most common and this was sure to be another one—a wounded sugar glider, an orphaned kangaroo, or perhaps an injured possum.

She was dead tired tonight, but now, before she could crawl into bed, she would have to attend to this.

She found the key, opened the front door and reached inside to turn on the porch light. Behind her, Will was waiting at the front gate and she sent him a friendly wave. 'Thanks for the lift,' she called.

He returned her wave and she watched as he headed back to the truck, then, with the flowers in one arm, she picked up the sack. The animal inside wriggled, which was a good sign. Maybe it wasn't too badly hurt and she wouldn't lose too much sleep tonight.

She heard her dogs scratching at the back door, but they

would have to wait a bit longer for her attention. She took the sack through to the surgery, put the roses and lilies in one of the huge metal sinks and set the bag down gently on the metal examining table.

First things first, she kicked off her shoes. That was *so-o-o-o* much better. Yawning widely, she unknotted the string around the neck of the bag.

A snake's head shot out.

Lucy screamed.

Panic flooded her!

A snake was the last thing she'd expected. The worst thing. She loved animals. She loved all animals. But she still couldn't help being terrified of snakes.

Her heart leapt in a rush of instinctive primeval terror. She couldn't deal with this.

Not now. Not alone in the middle of the night.

Paralysed by fear, she thought of Will driving off in his truck and seriously considered chasing after him, yelling for help. She whimpered his name and was ready to scream again when footsteps thundered up the path and Will appeared at the surgery doorway.

'Lucy, what's the matter?'

'A s-snake!' With a shaking hand she pointed to the sack.

'Let me deal with it.' He spoke calmly and, just like that, he crossed the floor to the wriggling hessian bag.

Lucy watched, one hand clamped over her mouth to hold back another scream, as Will carefully pulled the top of the sack apart, then, with commendable cool, gripped the snake firmly, just behind its head.

'It's a carpet python,' he told her smoothly as he lifted it out and took hold of the tail, while the snake thrashed wildly. 'And it's wounded.'

A carpet python.

Right. Lucy drew a deep breath. Her racing heartbeats subsided. Carpet pythons weren't poisonous. Actually, now that she was calming down, she could see the distinctive brown and cream markings on the snake's back.

'I'm afraid I panicked,' she said. 'Someone left the bag on my porch and I was expecting a small motherless furry creature.'

'Instead you have an angry snake with a nasty gash on its back.' The expression in Will's grey eyes was both tender and amused.

No longer trembling, Lucy came closer and saw the wound halfway down the snake's length. 'I'm afraid snakes are the one species of the animal kingdom I find hard to love. But this fellow's actually quite beautiful, isn't he?'

'As snakes go—he's extremely handsome,' Will said dryly. 'What do you want to do with him? Would you try to treat a wound like this?'

'I can at least clean it up. Maybe give it a few stitches.'

'Can you leave it till tomorrow? Shall I put it in a cage for you?'

She bit back a sigh and shook her head. 'The biggest threat for him is infection, so I really should see to the wound straight away.' Shooting Will an apologetic glance, she said, 'It won't take long, but I'm afraid I couldn't possibly manage without an assistant.'

He chuckled. 'No problem. I'm all yours.'

The sparkle in his eyes sent heat flaming in her cheeks. Tightly, she said, 'Thank you. If you'll keep holding him right there, I'll get organised. First, I'm going to have to feed oxygen and anaesthetic down his trachea.'

'You're going to knock him out just to clean up a wound?'

'It's the only way to keep a snake still. They're actually very sensitive to pain.'

As Lucy set up the gas cylinders, her mind raced ahead, planning each step of the procedure. She would place a wooden board between the python and the metal table to keep him that little bit warmer. And she needed something to hold the wounded section steady while she worked on it. Masking tape would do the least damage to the python's sensitive skin.

Quickly she assembled everything she needed— scissors, scalpels, tweezers, swabs, needles—and then she donned sterile gloves. 'OK, let's get this gas into him.'

Will held the snake's head steady while she fed the tube down its mouth, and she was amazed that she wasn't scared any more.

'How many pythons' lives have you saved?' Will asked as they waited for the anaesthetic to take effect.

'This is the first.'

He smiled. 'I can remember your very first patient.'

She frowned at him, puzzled. 'You were in Argentina when I started to work as a vet.'

'Before that. Don't you remember the chicken you brought to school in a woolly sock?'

'Oh, yes.' She grinned. 'The poor little thing hatched on a very cold winter's morning and I was worried that it wouldn't make it through the day.'

'You kept it hidden under the desk.'

'Until Mr Sanderson discovered it during biology and turned it into a lecture on imprinting.'

Their eyes met and they smiled and for a heady moment, Lucy was sixteen again and Will Carruthers was…

No, for heaven's sake.

Shocked by how easily she was distracted by him, she centred her thoughts on cleaning the outside of the python's wound with alcohol wipes and foaming solution. Then, when her patient was completely under, she began to debride the damaged tissue.

All the time she worked, Will was silent, watching her with a curious smile that she tried very hard to ignore.

'I guess this isn't quite how you expected to spend your evening,' she said as she finally began to suture the delicate skin together.

'Wouldn't have missed this for the world.' He chuckled softly. 'You have to admit, it's a unique experience. How many guys have watched a barefoot bridesmaid stitch up a python at midnight?'

Lucy couldn't help smiling. 'You make it sound like some kind of medieval witches' ritual.'

'The rites of spring?'

'Maybe, but then again, how many vets have been assisted by a hun—a guy in best man's clobber?'

Lucy thanked heavens she'd retracted the word *hunk*. For heaven's sake. It was the dinner suit factor. Stick the plainest man in a tuxedo and his looks were improved two hundred per cent. Will in a tuxedo was downright dangerous.

But she was grateful for his help. Working side by side with him again, she'd felt good in a weirdly unsettled-yet-comfortable way. They'd always worked well together.

'You're a tough cookie,' Will told her. 'You were white as a ghost and shaking when I came in and yet you morphed into a steady-handed snake surgeon.'

'It's my job,' she said, trying not to look too pleased.

She dropped the suture needles into the tray and snapped off her sterile gloves, removed the paper apron and rolled up the disposable sheet she'd used to drape over the wound.

'So where will we put this fellow while he sleeps off his ordeal?' Will asked.

'He'll have to go in one of the cages out the back.' Carefully, she peeled away the masking tape that had kept the snake straight.

'Shall I do the honours?'

'Thanks, Will. There's a cage in the far corner, away from the other patients. If you give me a minute, I'll line it with thick newspaper to keep him warm and dry.'

By the time the python was safely in its cage it was long past midnight but, to Lucy's surprise, she didn't feel tired any more. She tried to tell herself that she'd found working on a completely new species exhilarating, but she knew very well it had everything to do with Will's presence.

She'd felt relaxed and focused and it had been like stepping back in time to their student days. But, dear heaven, it was such a long time ago and they couldn't really go back, could they?

'Let's go through to the kitchen,' she said once they'd cleaned up.

She snapped the kitchen light on and the room leapt to life. She was rather proud of the renovations she'd made to this room, painting the walls a soft buttercup and adding hand painted tiles to the splashback over the sink. And she'd spent ages hunting for the right kind of cupboards and shelving in country-style second-hand shops.

'I'd better let the boys in.'

As soon as Lucy opened the back door, Seamus and Harry bounded inside, greeting her with doggy kisses and fiercely wagging tails, as if she'd been away for six months.

At last the dogs calmed down and she turned to Will. 'I think you've earned a drink.'

'I believe I have,' he agreed and he immediately began to remove his jacket and tie.

Lucy drew a sharp breath, already doubting the soundness of this idea. But she couldn't send Will packing after he'd been so helpful. Surely two old friends could have a drink together?

'What are you in the mood for?' *Oh, cringe. What a question.* 'Alcohol or coffee?' she added quickly.

She opened the fridge. 'If you'd like alcohol, I'm afraid there's only beer or white wine.'

Will chose beer and Lucy poured a glass of wine for herself. She found a wedge of Parmesan cheese and freshly shelled walnuts and set them on a platter with crackers and slices of apple.

'Come on through to the lounge room,' she said. 'It's pretty shabby, though. I started renovating the kitchen and then ran out of enthusiasm.'

Tonight, however, Lucy was surprised. She hadn't drawn the curtains and the lounge room, now flooded by moonlight, had taken on a strangely ethereal beauty. The shabbiness had all but disappeared and the garish colours of the cotton throws she'd used to cover the tattered upholstery had taken on a subtle glow.

'I might leave the lights off,' she said. 'This room is definitely improved by moonlight.'

'Everything's improved by moonlight.'

She studiously ignored this comment in the same way that she avoided the sofa and flopped into a deep, comfy single chair instead.

With a be-my-guest gesture she directed Will to the

other chair. Then, as the dogs settled on the floor, heads on paws, niggles of disquiet returned to haunt her. It was such a long time since she and Will had been alone like this.

'Try some Parmesan and apple,' she said, diving for safety by offering him the plate. 'Have you tried them together? It's a nice combination.'

Will obliged and made appropriately, appreciative noises.

Lucy took a sip of wine. In many ways this was one of her favourite fantasies—talking to Will late into the night. But in the fantasies there'd been no awkwardness. They had been as comfortable and relaxed as they were ten years ago, before they'd drifted apart.

Lucy wondered what they would discuss now. Will had hinted that he had specific things he wanted to talk about. Would he raise them now? She wasn't sure she was ready to hear his thoughts on marriage and babies and being over the hill.

Perhaps he still felt that tonight wasn't the night to be deep and meaningful. She searched for a safe topic that didn't include weddings, or honeymoons, or babies.

'So, have you started hunting for a new job?' she asked.

'I haven't put in any applications yet.' Will settled more comfortably into his chair, crossed an ankle over a knee. 'But I've found a few positions I might apply for. There's even one in Armidale, at the university.'

'In Armidale?' So close? To cover her surprise, Lucy said, 'I have trouble picturing you as an academic behind a desk.'

He shrugged. 'I thought it would make a nice change, after years of hiking over deserts and mountains looking for rocks.'

'There's that, I guess.' She couldn't resist adding facetiously, 'I suppose geology is a young man's job.'

Will smiled into his glass, took a swig, then set it down.

'I imagine your parents would like you to take up farming,' she suggested.

'They've never mentioned it.' He sighed. 'They're actually talking about selling up.'

'Really?' Lucy stared at him, horrified.

'My mother's been bitten by the travel bug.'

'She must have caught it from you.'

Will smiled crookedly. 'Perhaps.'

'But your family's been farming Tambaroora for five generations.'

'And now they've come to the end of the line,' Will said dryly.

Nervous now, Lucy chewed at her lower lip. Already they were treading on sensitive ground. Everyone in the district had always known that Will's older brother, Josh, was expected to take over the family farm.

Josh's death had changed everything.

She closed her eyes, as if to brace herself for the slam of pain that she always felt when she thought about that time.

'We've never talked about it, Lucy.'

She didn't have to ask what Will meant. The fact that they had never really talked since Josh's death had been like an unhealed wound inside her. 'There wasn't any chance to talk,' she said defensively. 'You went away straight after the funeral.'

'There were lots of good reasons for me not to stay. Your father didn't help.'

'My father?'

'After Josh's funeral, I tried to phone. I turned up on your doorstep, but your father wouldn't let me near you.'

Lucy stared at Will, stunned. 'I didn't know that.' Her

eyes stung and she blinked back tears. If she'd known Will had called, what would she have done? What might have been different?

Will's shoulders lifted in a shrug. 'Your father was probably right to protect you. I...I can't imagine that I would have been much help at the time.'

Lucy swallowed to ease the aching lump in her throat. She'd been in a terrible state after the funeral and the miscarriage. The really awful thing was that everyone thought she was grieving, and she was, of course, but a huge part of her distress had been caused by her overpowering feelings of guilt. 'Did you know...about the baby?'

'Gina told me at the time,' Will said quietly. And then, after a beat, 'I'm really sorry, Lucy.'

He sounded almost too apologetic, as if somehow he felt responsible. But that didn't make sense.

Lucy willed her hand to stop trembling as she held out the plate to him and he made a selection. For some time they sat in silence, nibbling walnuts in the silvered half-light, and then Will changed the subject.

'You've done so well here,' he said. 'I'm hearing from everyone that you're a fabulous vet.'

'I love my job.'

Will nodded, then he asked carefully, 'So you're happy, Lucy?'

From force of habit, a lie leapt to her lips. 'Of course.' She reached down and patted Harry's silky black and white head. 'I'm perfectly happy. I love this district. I love my work.'

'But is it enough?'

Oh, help. Lucy covered her dismay with a snappy reply. 'What kind of question is that?'

'An important one.'

'You answer it then.' She knew she sounded tense, but she couldn't help it. Will's question unnerved her. It was too searching, too close to a truth she didn't want to reveal. 'Are you happy, Will? Is your work enough?'

'Not any more.'

It wasn't the answer she'd expected and she took a moment to digest it. 'I suppose that's why you're looking for something different?'

'I suppose it is.' He circled the rim of his glass with his finger. 'I've had a bit of a wake up call.'

A swift flare of shock ripped through Lucy like a sniper's gunshot. 'Will, you're not sick, are you?'

'No, thank God, but I've had a close shave. I haven't told my family this. I didn't want to upset them, but there was an explosion in an old mine we were surveying.'

'In Mongolia?'

'Yes.' His face was suddenly tight and strained. 'The two men with me were both killed. Right in front of me. I've no idea how I escaped with a few scratches and bruises.'

'Oh, God, Will, that's terrible.' Tears threatened again as Lucy tried not to think the unthinkable—that there had almost been a world where Will didn't exist.

'I went to their funerals,' Will said quietly. 'And they really opened my eyes.'

'In what way?'

In the moonlight, she could see the sober intensity in Will's face.

'Barney was a bachelor, you see. No ties. So his funeral was a simple gathering of family and friends. There were a few words to say he was a good bloke and then a rather boozy wake. But Keith was a family man, always talking about his wife and three kids. And at the funeral his son spoke.'

Will sighed and rubbed at his forehead. 'He was such a courageous little guy. He couldn't have been more than ten years old. And he stood up there in front of us, with these big brown eyes, shiny with tears. His voice was all squeaky and threatening to break, but he told us all how proud he was of his father and how he wanted to live his life in a way that would go on making his dad proud.'

Lucy's throat ached at the thought of that little boy. She could picture his mother, too. The poor woman would have been so proud, despite her grief.

'I can't stop thinking about that kid,' Will said. 'He was like this fantastic gift to the world that Keith had left behind.'

Lucy reached for the handkerchief she'd tucked into the bodice of her dress and dabbed at her eyes.

'I'm sorry,' Will said. 'I'm being maudlin, talking about funerals when we've just been to a wedding.'

'No, it's OK.' She sniffed and sent him a watery smile. 'It's just happened to you, so of course it's on your mind. Anyway, that's what life's all about, isn't it? Births, deaths and marriages.'

He smiled sadly. 'I guess I'm a slow learner. It wasn't till I was sitting in that church that I suddenly got it. I could finally understand why Gina went to so much trouble to have a family, and why Mattie was prepared to undergo something so amazingly challenging as a surrogate pregnancy.'

'Yes,' Lucy said, but the single word came out too loud and sounded more like a sob.

The dogs lifted their heads and made soft whining noises in her direction. With a cry of dismay, Will lurched to his feet.

'I'm so sorry,' he said. 'I should be more sensitive. I shouldn't be burdening you with this.'

He was referring to her miscarriage. Would he be shocked to hear that she still longed for a baby, that her need was bordering on obsession?

With an angry shake of his head, he went to the window, thrust his hands into his trouser pockets and looked out into the night.

Despite her tension, Lucy was mesmerised by the sight of him limned by moonlight. Her eyes feasted on his profile, on his intelligent forehead, on the decisive jut of his nose, his strong chin with its appealing cleft.

Without looking at her, he said, 'I'm surprised you haven't found someone else and settled down to start a family.'

Oh, help. Lucy stiffened. Again, Will had gone too far. Again, her chin lifted in defence and she hit back. 'I could say the same about you.'

'Ah.' He turned back from the window. His eyes shimmered and he said in a dry tone, 'But I'm the vagabond and you're the homebody.'

Too true.

However, Lucy couldn't help remembering how he'd come rushing back to Australia when she and Josh had announced their engagement.

She'd always wondered why.

But there was no way she could open up that discussion now. Not tonight.

She felt too vulnerable tonight and she was scared she might blurt out something she'd regret later. It would be too embarrassing and shameful to confess that she'd finally gone out with Will's brother, hoping that word would reach Will and spark a reaction.

If she told him that, she'd also have to confess that the plan had backfired when she'd become pregnant.

It was more than likely she would never be able to talk to Will about this.

Nevertheless, tonight's conversation felt like an important step. It was almost as if she and Will had picked up their friendship where they'd left off. He'd told her about the funeral, something he hadn't been able to share with his family.

It suddenly felt OK to say, 'I've actually become quite desperate to have a baby.'

Will spun around from the window and his chest rose and fell. Above his open white shirt, the muscles in his throat rippled. His eyes smouldered in the cool white light. 'You'd make a wonderful mother, Lucy.'

The compliment made her want to cry, but she gave him a shrugging smile. 'It's a terrible waste, isn't it?'

She hadn't expected to say more but, now that she'd started, it was surprisingly easy to keep going. 'To be honest, I worry constantly about the state of my ovaries and whether I can expect them to go on delivering, month after month.'

'The old biological clock?'

She nodded. 'Early menopause runs in my family. That's why I'm an only child.'

Will frowned. 'But I have it on good authority that you've turned down at least three proposals of marriage.'

Heat flooded Lucy's face. 'I suppose Gina told you that?'

He nodded.

'OK, so I'm fussy, but that's because I'm not so desperate that I'd settle for just any guy as a husband. Willowbank isn't exactly swarming with Mr Rights, you know. I'd rather be a single mother.'

Abruptly, Will came back to his chair and sank down

into it, long legs stretching in front of him. 'Why would you want to be a single mother?'

'Because it's better than not being a mother at all.'

He looked surprised and thoughtful.

Lucy made herself comfortable with her legs curled and an elbow propped on the chair's arm, her cheek resting on her hand. 'I've been to a fertility clinic,' she told Will. 'And I've already tried one round of IVF.'

'IVF?' he repeated, sounding shocked.

'Why not?'

'Isn't that a bit…extreme?'

'It seemed logical to me. I've inseminated hundreds of animals and it worked beautifully for Mattie and Gina. But, unfortunately, it didn't work for me.'

Will made a soft sound, a kind of strangled gasp.

'I'm sorry. That's probably too much information,' she said.

But Will shook his head and, a moment later, a smile played around his lips. He tapped at the arm of his chair. 'It's a pity Mattie can't have a baby for you.'

Lucy knew he was joking and forced a weak laugh. Uncurling her legs, she sat straight in her chair. 'Don't worry, that thought's occurred to me but I imagine Mattie has other plans now she has a husband.'

'I'm sure she has.' With a thoughtful frown, Will scratched at his jaw. 'But it's a pity there isn't someone who could help you out.'

'Do you mean a good friend? Someone like you, Will?'

CHAPTER FIVE

LUCY could not believe she'd just said that.

What had she been thinking?

How on earth could she have boldly suggested that Will could help her to have a baby—out of friendship?

What must he think of her?

The only sound in the room came from Seamus, the Irish setter, snoring softly at Will's feet. Lucy stared at the sleeping dog while her heart beat crazily.

'You know that was a joke, don't you?' she said in a small voice.

To her dismay, Will didn't answer and she wished she could crawl away and hide with her tail between her legs, the way Seamus and Harry did when they were in big trouble.

If only she could press a rewind button and take those words back.

When the silence became unbearable she looked up and saw Will's serious expression and her heart juddered. 'Will, I didn't mean it. It was my warped sense of humour. You know I've never been very good at making jokes. They always come out wrong. I'm sorry. Honestly, I feel so embarrassed.'

He looked shaken. 'For a moment there, I thought you were serious.'

'I wasn't, Will. You can calm down.'

Suddenly a cloud covered the moon and the room was plunged in darkness. Lucy turned on the lamp beside her and the return of light seemed to clear the air.

Will rose abruptly and stood towering over her. 'Perhaps I'd better get going before I say something outrageous, too.'

As Lucy stood she prayed that her legs were steady enough to support her. 'Thanks for helping me with the python,' she remembered to say as they crossed the lounge room.

Will smiled. 'My pleasure. I hope he makes a good recovery, and thanks for the drink and the chat. It was like old times.'

No, Lucy thought. Blurting out her desire to have a baby was not remotely like old times.

They went through to the kitchen, where Will collected his jacket and tie, and then on to the front door. His hand touched Lucy's shoulder and she jumped.

'See you later, Goose.' He dropped a light kiss on her cheek and then he was gone.

Will felt as if he'd stepped off a roller coaster as he started up the truck and drove away, watching the lights of Lucy's house grow smaller and more distant in the rearvision mirror.

What a crazy night! In a matter of hours, he'd gone from being best man at a wedding to standing in as a veterinary nurse to fielding a request for his services as a father for Lucy's baby.

Not that Lucy had been serious, of course.

But bloody hell. The thought gripped Will and frightened him beyond belief. His heart had almost raced out of control when Lucy made that offhand suggestion tonight.

He was still shaken now, even though the subject had been laid to rest. Problem was, he couldn't let it go.

He kept thinking about how badly she wanted a baby. If he hadn't seen the emotional pain that Gina had been through, or if he hadn't so recently attended Keith's funeral, he might not have caught the genuine longing in Lucy's voice. In her eyes.

He might not have understood, might have simply thought she was selfish, wanting it all, when she already had so much.

But now he got it, he really understood that the desire to have a child came from somewhere deep, so deep that it couldn't be properly explained. And it shouldn't be ignored.

But should he be involved? For Pete's sake, he'd seen the haunted loneliness in Lucy's eyes and he'd almost grabbed her suggestion and moulded it into a realistic option.

They'd been such good friends and he'd wanted to help her.

But father her baby?

That was even crazier than the way he'd felt when he'd danced with her tonight at the wedding. It was the kiss on the veranda revisited. He'd been caught out by unexpected emotions, by an inappropriate desire to get too close to Lucy.

Every time she'd stumbled against him, he'd wanted to keep her close. He'd wanted to inhale the clean, rosy scent of her skin, to touch his lips to her skin, right there, in front of the wedding guests.

Thank heavens he'd had the sense to stop dancing before things got out of hand.

But it didn't really make sense that he was feeling this way about Lucy now. Why would he want to play second fiddle to the memory of his brother?

If he'd wanted Lucy as his girlfriend, he should have grabbed the chance when they were at university, before she got to know Josh. Problem was, he'd been too distracted by the sheer numbers of girls at Sydney Uni and he'd wanted to play the field.

And, truth be told, when he thought about those days, he had to admit that whenever he'd made a move in Lucy's direction she'd adroitly held him at a distance. She'd insisted that she was his buddy, not his girlfriend.

And yet she'd fallen for Josh quite easily. Will knew that was exactly why he mustn't think twice about her crazy suggestion.

Lucy had loved his brother. She'd been about to marry his brother and have his brother's baby.

Did he honestly think he could make amends by stepping in as a substitute?

The question teased him as he steered the truck over a single lane wooden bridge that crossed Willow Creek. He felt the familiar sickening slug of guilt he always felt when he thought about Josh and remembered the row they had on that last fateful morning before he'd died.

That was what he should have talked about tonight. He should have confessed his role in Josh's death.

Oh, God. The mere thought of telling Lucy the truth caused a sickening jolt in his chest. She would hate him.

He couldn't take that risk.

The next day, Sunday, dragged for Lucy. She wasn't on call so, apart from checking on her patients, including the python, who was recovering nicely, she couldn't distract herself with work.

She collected her car from the Careys' and spent a happy half hour discussing the wedding with Mattie's mum over a cup of tea. In the afternoon, she took her dogs for a lovely long walk along Willow Creek, but they weren't good conversationalists, so she was left with far too much time to brood over the huge gaffe she'd made during last night's conversation with Will.

She couldn't believe she'd actually asked her school-girl crush to help her to have a baby. Talk about a Freudian slip!

What must Will think of her?

Why in heaven's name had she blurted out such a suggestion when she'd once been engaged to Will's brother?

The question brought her to a halt, standing at the edge of the creek, staring down into the clear running water. She remembered the happy times she'd spent here with Will, panning for gold or sapphires. How excited they'd been over the tiniest speck of gold or the smallest dull chips of dark glass that signified sapphires.

She'd never once let Will see how much she loved him. She'd been too scared to risk losing him by telling him how she felt.

She was so totally lost in thought that she was startled when her dogs began to bark suddenly.

'Stop that, Harry,' she called. 'Seamus, what's the matter?'

Then she heard the snap of twigs and the crunch of gravel underfoot. Someone was coming along the track.

'Come here,' Lucy ordered but, to her dismay, the dogs ignored her. Their tails kept wagging and they yapped expectantly as a tall figure came around the bend.

It was Will.

A flare of shock burst inside her, as if someone had lit a match. Will looked surprised too, but he seemed to recover more quickly. He smiled, while Lucy's heart continued to thump fretfully.

'Fancy seeing you here,' he drawled.

'I brought the dogs for a walk.'

He grinned and bent down to give the boys a quick scruff around the ears. 'I needed to get out of the house.'

'Already? But you've just arrived home.'

'I know.' His grey eyes sparkled as he looked up at her. 'But I've had this crazy idea rattling around in my head and I needed to get away to think.'

'Oh,' Lucy said uncertainly.

The dogs, content with Will's greeting, went back to hunting for the delectable smells in a nearby lantana bush. Watching them, Will said, 'I've been thinking about your baby proposal.'

'Will, it wasn't a proposal. You know I didn't mean it.'

With a distinct lack of haste, he said, 'But is it such a bad idea?'

Lucy's mouth fell open. Surely he wasn't serious? 'Of course it's a bad idea. It's crazy.'

He looked about him, letting his gaze take in the silent trees and sky, the smooth stepping stones crossing the creek. 'You really want a baby,' he said quietly. 'You said so last night, and you're worried you're running out of time.'

Now it was Lucy who didn't answer. She couldn't. Her heart had risen to fill her throat. She'd never dreamed for a moment that Will would take her flippant comment even halfway seriously.

He stood, blocking her way on the narrow track,

watching her carefully. 'I'm sure you'd prefer your baby's father to be someone you know.'

She still couldn't speak. Her hand lifted to the base of her throat as she tried to still the wild pulse that beat there.

Will pressed his point. 'I imagine a friend must be a better option than an unknown donor in a sperm bank.'

'But friends don't normally have babies together.'

She couldn't see his expression. He'd turned to pluck at a long grass stalk and it made a soft snapping sound.

'People accept all kinds of convenient family arrangements these days,' he said. 'The locals in Willowbank have accepted the idea of Mattie's surrogacy very well.'

'Well, yes. That's true.'

But, despite her silly dreams, Lucy couldn't imagine having a baby with Will. He'd never fancied her. And, even if he did, he was Josh's brother.

'Look, Lucy, don't get me wrong. I'm not pushing this, but I'm happy to talk it through.'

'Why?'

A slow smile warmed his eyes. 'We haven't talked for years and we used to be really good at it.'

Lucy felt a blush spread upwards from her throat. Her mind was spinning, grasping desperately at the idea of Will as her baby's father and then slipping away again, as if the thoughts were made of ice. 'But what exactly are you saying? That you would be willing to…um…donate sperm for another round of IVF?'

Surprise flared in his face. He tossed the grass stalk into the water. 'If that's what you want.'

'I…I don't know.'

'Of course, there's always the natural alternative. If you've had trouble with IVF, that shouldn't be ruled out.'

Lucy bit her lip to cover her gasp of dismay. She watched the grass float away, disappearing behind a rock. The dogs began to bark again. 'They're tired of this spot and they want to move on,' she told Will.

'Let's walk, then,' he suggested.

There was just enough room on the track for them to walk side by side, and it should have been relaxing to walk with Will beside the creek—like in the old days. But today an unsettling awareness zapped through Lucy. She was too conscious of Will's tall, rangy body. So close. Touching close.

She couldn't think straight. She was so tantalised by the idea of a baby, but how could she even talk about having a baby with Will when she'd never admitted that she'd always had a crush on him?

She didn't want to frighten him away, not now when he'd made such an amazing suggestion.

Dragging in a deep breath, she said, 'OK. Just say we did…um…give this some thought. How do you actually feel about becoming a father?'

She glanced at Will and saw his quick smile. 'To be honest, fatherhood has been well down on my wish list. But I guess I'm seeing it in a new light lately. I've been hit by the feeling that I've been wasting my life.'

'Because of the little boy at the funeral?'

'Yes, that little guy really got to me. But there've been other things too—like Gina's twins. They knocked me for six. They're so damn cute.'

'I know. I'm eaten up with envy every time I see them. But you haven't answered me. Would you really want to be my baby's father?'

Will stopped walking. 'I can't promise I'd be a terrific

help, Lucy. I don't even know where I'm going to be working yet, so there's not much chance I'd be a hands-on father. But, if you want to have a child, I'd certainly be ready to help.'

She was so surprised she found her thoughts racing ahead. 'I don't mind managing on my own. It's what I'd planned anyway.'

Will smiled. 'So what does that mean? Do you want to give this some serious thought?'

'I...I don't know.' She was feeling so dazed. 'I know I was the one who started this, but I never dreamed you'd take me up on it.'

Even as she said this, Lucy wished she'd sounded more positive. This was her dream, to have Will's baby. OK, maybe the dream also involved Will falling madly and deeply in love with her, but surely half a dream was better than none?

'But I guess there's no harm in thinking about it,' she said.

His eyes were very bright, watching her closely. 'I wasn't even expecting to see you today. There's no pressure to make a decision now. We should sleep on it. If we decide to go ahead, we can fine-tune the details later.'

'Fine-tune?'

'IVF versus the alternative,' he said without smiling.

The alternative.

This time Lucy's skin began to burn from the inside out. She hadn't even been able to dance with Will last night without getting upset. How on earth could she possibly make love with him without a gigantic emotional meltdown?

The very thought of becoming intimate with Will sent flames shooting over her skin. She began to tremble.

'There's no rush,' he said. 'I could be around here for a

while yet, and if I move to Armidale it's only a couple of hours away.'

Lucy frowned at him. 'Armidale?'

'The job I mentioned. At the university.'

Oh. She expelled air noisily.

'Look, we both need time to think about this, Lucy.' Will watched her dogs running impatiently back and forth, trying to urge her to get walking again. 'And I should head back now.'

'All right.'

'I'm glad I ran into you,' he said.

Lucy nodded.

'So you'll give this some thought?'

'Yes,' she said, but a shiver rushed over her skin and she wrapped her arms around her as she watched Will walk away.

At the bend in the track he turned back and lifted his hand to wave. Then he smiled. And kept walking.

He hadn't been totally crazy, Will told himself as he strode back along the track beside the creek. He hadn't committed to a full-on relationship with his brother's ex. He'd simply offered to help her to have a baby.

This was purely and simply about the baby.

The baby Lucy longed for.

But it meant he'd be a father and he really liked that idea.

He'd be able to watch the baby grow. He'd help out with finances—school fees, pony club, whatever the kid needed. And who knew? Maybe, some day in the future, the kid might take an interest in Tambaroora, if it still belonged to the Carruthers family.

But the big thing was, the lucky child would have Lucy as its mother.

If any woman deserved to be a mother, Lucy did.

Will had dated a lot of women, but he couldn't think of anyone who was more suitable than Lucy McKenty to be the mother of his child.

And it wasn't such a crazy situation. Being good friends with his baby's mother was a vast improvement on some of the unhappy broken family set-ups that he'd heard his workmates complain about.

But the details of the baby's conception caused a road bump.

Will came to a halt as he thought about that. He snagged another grass stalk and chewed at it thoughtfully.

Any way he looked at this situation, leaping into bed with Lucy McKenty was stretching the boundaries of friendship.

But it was highly unlikely that she would agree to sex. Apart from the fact that Will was the brother of the man she'd planned to marry, and setting their friendship issues aside, Lucy was a vet. She used IVF all the time in her practice and she was bound to look on it as the straightforward and practical solution.

Except that she'd tried the clinical route once and it hadn't worked.

Which brought him back to the alternative. With Lucy.

Damn. He could still remember their long ago kiss on the veranda.

He should have forgotten it by now. He'd tried so hard to forget, but he could remember every detail of those few sweet minutes—the way Lucy had felt so alive and warm in his arms, the way she'd smelled of summer and tasted of every temptation known to man.

Hell. There was no contest, was there?

IVF was most definitely their sanest, safest option.

* * *

Lucy was in a daze as she walked back to her ute. She couldn't believe Will had given her suggestion serious thought. It was astonishing that he was actually prepared to help her to have her baby.

She couldn't deny she was tempted.

Tempted? Heavens, she was completely sold on the whole idea of having a dear little baby fathered by Will.

It was the means to this end that had her in a dither.

Sex with Will was so totally not a good idea. The very thought of it filled her with foolish longings and multiple anxieties.

She'd loved Will for so long now, it was like a chronic illness that she'd learned to adjust to. But to sleep with him would be like dancing on the edge of a cliff. She would be terrified of falling.

If only IVF was simpler.

She'd hated the process last time. All the tests and injections and clinical procedures and then the huge disappointment of failure. Not to mention the expense and the fact that, if she wanted to try again, she'd have to go back on that long waiting list.

Oh, man. Her thoughts went round and round, like dairy cows on a milking rotator. One minute she rejected the whole idea of having Will's baby, the next she was desperately trying to find a way to make it happen.

Could it work?

Could it possibly work?

Lucy remembered again how she'd felt when she'd seen Will at the wedding rehearsal, standing at the front of the church with tiny Mia in his arms. Just thinking about it made her teary. He would be such a fabulous father.

She drove home, but when she was supposed to be preparing dinner she was still lost in reverie, going over and over the same well worn thoughts.

She found herself standing at her kitchen sink, thinking about Will again. Still. She caught sight of her reflection in the window and was shocked to see that she was cradling a tea towel as if it were a baby. And her face was wet with tears.

The picture cut her to the core and, in that moment, she knew she had no choice. She wanted Will's baby more than anything she'd ever wanted in her life.

That precious baby's existence was a hundred times more important than the method of its conception.

Tomorrow, she should tell Will she'd made a decision.

Early next morning, however, there was a telephone call.

'Is that the young lady vet?'

'Yes,' Lucy replied, crossing her fingers. Calls this early on a Monday morning usually meant trouble.

'This is Barney May,' the caller said. 'I need someone to come and look at my sheep. Four of them have gone lame on me.'

Lucy suppressed a sigh. Lame sheep usually meant foot abscesses or, worse still, footrot, which was highly contagious. There'd been plenty of rain this spring so the conditions were ripe for an outbreak. *Darn it.*

'Could you come straight away?' Barney asked. 'I don't want a problem spreading through my whole herd.'

'Hang on. I'll have to check my schedule.'

She scanned through the surgery's diary for the day's appointments. It was the usual assortment—small animals with sore ears or eyes or skin conditions; a few vaccinations and general health checks for new puppies and kittens—nothing that her assistant couldn't handle.

'I'll be there in about an hour,' she told Barney.

'Good, lass. You know where I live—about ten kilometres out of town, past the sale yards on the White Sands Road.'

An hour later Lucy knew the worst. The sheep indeed had footrot and it had spread from the neighbouring property via a broken fence.

After paring the hooves of the unlucky sheep and prescribing footbaths, she had to continue her inspection and, all too soon, she discovered more evidence that the disease was spreading beyond the Mays' property, thanks to another farmer who'd really let his fences go.

Which spelled potential disaster.

Without question, it would mean a full week of hard work for Lucy. Her assistant would have to man the surgery while she toured the district, visiting all the farms as she tried to gauge just how far the problem ranged.

Each night she was exhausted and when she arrived home she had to face the surgery work that her assistant couldn't handle. By the time she crawled into bed she was too tired to tackle a complicated phone call to Will.

And, because the Carruthers family farm was at the opposite end of the district from the initial footrot outbreak, it was Friday afternoon before she got to Tambaroora.

It was a beautiful property with wide open paddocks running down to the creek and a grand old sandstone homestead, bang in the centre, surrounded by a green oasis of gardens. Lucy could never think about Tambaroora without seeing the garden filled with summer colour and smelling roses, jasmine, lavender and rosemary.

By the time she arrived, Will and his father had already completed a thorough inspection of their herd and they reported that their sheep were in good condition, but Lucy still needed to make spot sample checks.

Will hefted the heavy beasts she selected with obvious ease, and he kept them calm while she examined their hooves. She'd been dealing with farmers all week and she knew he made a difficult task look incredibly easy.

'For someone who doesn't think of himself as a farmer, you handle sheep well,' she said.

'Will's surprised us,' his father commented wryly. 'We didn't think he had it in him.'

A smile twisted Will's mouth as his father trudged off to attend to a ewe that had recently delivered twin lambs.

'I meant it,' Lucy told him. 'Not all farmers are good at handling stock. You're a natural.'

He looked amused. 'Maybe I was just trying to impress you.'

She rolled her eyes, but that was partly to cover the attack of nerves she felt at the thought of telling him she'd reached a decision about the baby. Her stomach was as jumpy as a grasshopper in a jar as he helped her to gather up her gear, then walked beside her to her ute.

'Do you have to hurry away?' he asked as she stowed her things. 'I was hoping we could talk.'

'About the baby idea?' She spoke as casually as she could.

There was no one around, but Will lowered his voice. 'Yes, I've been thinking it over.'

Her heart jumped like a skittish colt and she searched his face, trying to guess what he was going to tell her. If he'd decided to scrap the baby idea, she wasn't sure she could bear the disappointment. She'd become totally entranced by the thought of their adorable infant and she'd convinced herself that this time it would work.

With Will as her baby's father, she was confident of success.

She could be a mother. At last.

She forced a smile and willed herself to speak calmly. 'So, what have you decided?'

CHAPTER SIX

WILL'S eyes were almost silver in the outdoor light, so beautiful they stole Lucy's breath. 'I'd like to go ahead,' he said. 'I think you should try for a baby.'

'Wow.'

'So, are you keen too?'

'I am, yes.'

He smiled. 'Why don't we go for a walk?' He nodded towards the dark line of trees at the far end of a long, shimmering paddock of grain.

'Down by the creek again?' she asked, smiling.

'Why not?'

Why not, indeed? It had always been *their* place.

As Lucy walked beside Will, they chatted about her busy week and she tried to stay calm, to take in the special beauty of the late afternoon.

Cicadas were humming in the grass and the sinking sun cast a pretty bronzed glow over the wheat fields.

She tried to take in the details—the tracks that ants had made in an old weathered fence post, the angle of the shadows that stretched like velvet ribbons across the paddocks.

She really needed to stay calm.

It was ridiculous to be so churned up just talking to Will,

but now that they'd agreed to go ahead with this baby plan they had to discuss the more delicate details, like the method of conception.

How exactly did a girl tell a truly gorgeous man she'd fancied for years that she'd carefully weighed up the pros and cons and had decided, on balance, to have sex with him?

As they neared the creek she saw two wedge-tailed eagles hovering over a stick nest that they'd woven in the fork of a dead tree.

'I hope they don't plan to dine on our lambs,' Will said, watching them.

She might have replied, but they'd reached the shelter of the trees and her stomach was playing leapfrog with her heart.

It was so quiet down here. Too quiet. This part of the creek formed a still and silent pool and now, in the late afternoon, the birds had stopped calling and twittering. It seemed as if the whole world had stopped and was waiting to listen in to Lucy and Will's conversation.

'We need rain,' Will said as they came to a halt on the creek bank. 'The water level's dropping.'

Rain? How could he talk about rain? 'Now you're talking like a farmer.'

He pulled a comical face. 'Heaven forbid.'

Lucy drew a tense breath. 'Will, about the fine-tuning—'

'Lucy, I think you're probably right—'

They had both started talking at the same moment and now they stopped. Their gazes met and they laughed self-consciously.

'You first,' Will said.

'No, you tell me what you were going to say. What am I right about?'

'IVF. I know it's what you'd prefer and I think we should go that route.'

'Really?'

Oh, heavens. She hadn't sounded disappointed, had she?

Will's blue shirt strained at the shoulder seams as he shrugged. 'I can understand that it makes total sense to you and I'm prepared to do whatever's necessary.'

Lucy gulped as she took this in.

He watched her with a puzzled smile. 'I thought you'd be pleased.'

'Oh, I…I am. Yes, I'm really happy.' In truth, she couldn't believe the piercing sense of anticlimax she felt. 'I'm just surprised,' she said, working hard to cover her ridiculous disappointment. 'I spent the whole week worrying that you were going to back out altogether.'

Dropping her gaze to the ground, she hooked her thumbs into the back pockets of her jeans and kicked at a loose stone.

'So what were you going to say about the fine-tuning?' Will asked.

Lucy's face flamed. Now that Will had agreed to IVF, there was no point in telling him her decision. He'd never fancied her in that way, so it would be a huge challenge to become intimate.

'Lucy?'

'It doesn't matter now.'

'Why not?' Will swallowed abruptly and his eyes burned her.

'Honestly, Will, it's really great that you'd like to help with IVF. I'm very grateful. I couldn't be more pleased.'

His grey eyes were searching her, studying her. Suddenly they narrowed thoughtfully and then widened with surprise. 'Don't tell me you'd come around to…to the other option?'

'No, no. If you want to use IVF, that's good,' she said.

'I didn't exactly say it's what I *want*.' A nervous smile flickered in his face, then vanished. 'I was trying to look at this from your point of view. I thought it's what you'd prefer.'

'Thanks, Will. I appreciate that.' Lucy bit her lip to stop herself from saying more.

He stood very still, his hands hanging loosely at his sides, and she knew he was watching her while she continued to avoid his gaze.

'Or are you actually worried about IVF?' he asked cautiously. 'I know it didn't work for you last time.'

Lucy drew a sharp breath, and let it out slowly. Without meeting his gaze, she said, 'I can't say I'm in love with the idea of going through all those clinical procedures again.'

'The alternative is much simpler.'

'In some ways.' She knew her face must be turning bright pink.

To her surprise, Will looked as worried as she felt. He pointed to a smooth shelf of shady rock hanging over the water. 'Look, why don't we sit down for a bit?'

'Very well,' she agreed rather primly.

Despite the shade from overhead trees, the rock still held some of the day's warmth and they sat with their feet dangling over the edge, looking down into the green, still water. They'd sat like this many times, years ago, when they were school friends.

How innocent those days seemed now.

A childish chant from Lucy's schooldays taunted her. *First comes love, then comes marriage, then comes Lucy with a baby carriage.*

Now she and Will were putting an entirely new spin on that old refrain.

She picked up a fallen leaf and rolled it against her thigh, making a little green cylinder. 'Are we mad, Will? Is it crazy for us to be trying for a baby without love or marriage?'

She sensed a sudden vibrating tension in him, saw his Adam's apple slide up and down in his throat. He picked up a small stone and lobbed it into the water. 'I don't think it's a crazy idea. Not if you're quite sure it's what you want.'

She let the leaf uncurl. 'I definitely want to have a baby, and I really like the idea of having you as the father.' She rolled the leaf again into a tight little cylinder.

'But sex is a problem,' Will suggested and his voice was rough and gravelly, so that the statement fell between them like the stone he'd dropped in the water.

'It could be.' Lucy concentrated on the leaf in her hand.

'I know I'm not Josh,' Will said quietly.

Her head jerked up. With a stab of guilt, she realised she hadn't been thinking about Josh at all. Poor Will. Did he think he had to live up to some romantic ideal set by his brother?

If only he knew the truth.

But if she told him how she really felt about him, he might be more worried than ever.

No, this rather unconventional baby plan would actually work best if they approached it as friends.

Lucy looked down at Will's hand as it rested against the rock. It was a strong workmanlike hand, with fine sun-bleached hairs on the back. She placed her hand on top of his. 'I don't want you to be like Josh,' she said.

His throat worked.

'But this might be too hard,' she said. 'Friends don't usually jump into bed together.'

'But they might,' he said gently, 'if it was a means to an end. The best means to a good end.'

She sucked in a breath, looked up at the sky.

The best means to a good end.

A baby.

'That's a nice way of putting it,' she said, already picturing the sweet little baby in her arms. Oh, heavens, she could almost feel the warm weight of it, feel its head nestled in the crook of her arm, see its tiny hands. Would they be shaped like Will's?

'So what do you think?' he asked.

Lucy nodded thoughtfully. 'You're right. It's a means to an end.' After a bit, she said, 'It would probably be best if we took a strictly medical approach.'

Will frowned. 'Medical?'

'I can get ovulation predictors.' She was gaining confidence now. 'I'll need to let you know exactly when I'm ovulating.'

His eyes widened in surprise.

'You do know there are only a very few days each month when a woman is fertile, don't you?'

'Ah, yes, of course,' he said, recovering quickly. He sent her a puzzled smile. 'So what happens when it's all systems go? Will you send me a text message?' His smile deepened. 'Or fly a green flag above your door?'

Lucy saw his smile and she felt a massive chunk of tension flow out of her. To her surprise, she found herself smiling too. 'Oh, why don't I just go the whole hog and place a notice in the Post Office window?'

Now Will was chuckling. 'Better still, you could take out a full page ad in the *Willowbank Chronicle*.'

Suddenly, it was just like old times. Laughter had always been a hallmark of their friendship.

'What about hiring Frank Pope, the crop duster?' Lucy suggested. 'He's a dab hand at sky-writing. Can't you just see it written in the sky? Will Carruthers, tonight's the night.'

Laughing with her, Will scratched at his jaw. 'That's a bit too personal. What about a subtle message in code?'

'All right…let me see…something like…the hen is broody?'

'In your case it would have to be the Goose.'

Lucy snorted. 'Oh, yes. A broody goose.'

She collapsed back onto the rock, laughing.

Their conversation was ridiculous, but it was so therapeutic to be able to joke about such a scary subject.

Her anxiety was still there, just under the surface, but she felt much better as she lay on the warm rock, still chuckling as she looked up at the sky through a lacework of green branches.

She and Will would have to stay relaxed if this plan was to have any chance of working. Perhaps everything would be all right if they could both keep their sense of humour.

Will's mobile phone rang a week later, when he was sitting at the breakfast table with his parents. Quickly, he checked the caller ID, saw Lucy's name and felt a jolting thud in the centre of his chest.

'Excuse me,' he mumbled, standing quickly. 'I'll take this outside.'

His heart thumped harder than a jackhammer as he went out onto the back porch, letting the flyscreen door swing shut behind him.

'Good morning.' His voice was as rough as sandpaper.

'Will, it's Lucy.'

'Hi. How are you?'

'Fine, thanks.'

There was an awkward pause—a stilted silence broken only by a kookaburra's laughter and the whistle from the kettle in the kitchen as it came to the boil. Will's heartbeats drummed in his ears.

Lucy said, 'I was wondering if you were free to come to dinner tonight.'

'Tonight?'

'Yes, would that be OK?'

Will was shaking, which was crazy. This entire past week had been crazy. He'd been on tenterhooks the whole time, waiting for Lucy's call. He'd actually lent a hand with drenching the sheep, much to his father's amazement. He'd enjoyed the work, even though he'd originally made the offer simply to keep himself busy, to take his mind off Lucy.

'Sure,' he said now, walking further from the house, out of his parents' earshot. 'Dinner would be great. I'll bring a bottle of wine. What would you prefer? White or red?'

'Well, I'm making lasagne, so perhaps red?'

'Lasagne? Wow.' As far as he could remember, cooking had never been Lucy's forte. Perhaps she'd taken a course? 'Red it is, then.'

'See you around seven?'

'I'll be there.' And then, because he couldn't help it, 'Goose?'

'Yes?'

'Is this—?'

'Yes,' she said quickly before he could find the right words. Will swallowed. 'OK, then. See you at seven.'

He strolled back into the kitchen, body on fire, affecting a nonchalance he was far from feeling.

'I won't be home for dinner this evening,' he told his parents.

His mother smiled. 'So you're going out? That's nice, dear. It's good to see you catching up with your old friends.' She was always happy when she thought he was seeing someone. She'd never given up hope of more grandchildren.

Will's father looked more puzzled than pleased. This was the longest stretch his son had spent at home since he'd left all those years ago. Will knew they were both surprised, and expecting that he would take off again at a moment's notice.

But Gina and Tom's babies were to be christened as soon as Mattie and Jake returned from their honeymoon, so it was an excellent excuse for him to stay on.

As he tackled the remainder of his bacon and eggs he wondered what his parents would think if they knew he planned to help Lucy McKenty to become pregnant before he headed away again.

Half an hour before Will's expected arrival, Lucy's kitchen looked like a crime site, splattered from end to end with tomato purée and spilt milk, eggshells and flour.

She wanted everything to be so perfect for tonight and she'd actually had a brand-new whizz-bang stove installed. She'd even taken a whole afternoon off work to get this dinner ready for Will.

So far, however, the only part of the meal that looked edible was the pineapple poached in rum syrup, which was precisely one half of the dessert.

How on earth had she thought she could manage stewed

fruit and a baked custard as well as lasagne? She'd never been much of a cook and these dishes were so fiddly.

But now—*thank heavens*—everything was finally in the oven, although she still had to clean up the unholy mess and have a shower and change her clothes and put on make-up and set the table. She'd meant to hunt in the garden for flowers for the table as well, but the dinner preparations had taken her far too long.

She was never going to be ready in time.

Guys never noticed flowers anyway.

In a hectic whirl she dashed about the kitchen, throwing rubbish into plastic bags, wiping bench tops and spills on the floor, hurling everything else pell-mell into the dishwasher to be stacked again properly later.

Later.

Oh, heavens, she mustn't think about that.

The only good thing about being so frantically busy was that it had helped her not to dwell too deeply on the actual reason for this dinner. The merest thought of what was supposed to happen *after* the meal set off explosions inside her, making her feel like a string of firecrackers at Chinese New Year.

Hastily Lucy showered, slathering her skin with her favourite jasmine-scented gel and checking that her waxed legs were still silky and smooth.

Her hair was short so she simply towelled it dry, threw in a little styling product and let it do its own thing.

She put on a dress. She spent her working life in khaki jeans and she didn't wear dresses very often, but this one was pretty—a green and white floral slip with shoestring straps and tiny frills around the low V neckline. It suited her. She felt good in it.

A couple of squirts of scent, a dab of lip gloss, a flourish with the mascara brush…

A truck rumbled to a growling halt outside.

Lucy froze.

Her reflection in the bedroom mirror blushed and her skin flashed hot and cold. Frenzied butterflies beat frantic wings in her stomach.

Firm footsteps sounded on the front path and her legs became distinctly wobbly. This was crazy.

It's only Will, not Jack the Ripper.

Unfortunately, this thought wasn't as calming as it should have been.

Concentrate on the meal. First things first. One step at a time.

It was no good. She was still shaking as she opened the door.

Will was dressed casually, in blue jeans and an open-necked white shirt with the sleeves rolled up to just below the elbow. Behind him, the twilight shadows were the deepest blue. He was smiling. He looked gorgeous—with the kind of masculine fabulousness that smacked a girl between the eyes.

'Nice dress,' he said, smiling his appreciation.

'Thanks.'

With a pang Lucy allowed herself a rash moment of fantasy in which Will was her boyfriend and madly in love with her, planning to share a future with her and the baby they hoped to make.

Just as quickly she wiped the vision from her thoughts. Over the past ten years she'd had plenty of practice at erasing that particular dream.

Reality, her reality, was a convenient and practical parenting agreement. There was simply no point in hoping for more. She was incredibly grateful for Will's offer. It was her best, quite possibly her only prospect for motherhood.

'Something smells fantastic,' he said.

'Thanks.' Her voice was two levels above a whisper. 'I hope it tastes OK. Come on in.'

She'd planned to eat in the kitchen, hoping that the room's rustic simplicity and familiar cosiness would help her to stay calm.

Already, that plan had flown out of the window. She was almost sick with nerves.

'Take any seat, Will.' She gestured towards chairs gathered around the oval pine table. 'You can open the wine if you like. I'd better check the dinner.'

She opened the oven door. *Concentrate on the food.*

Her heart sank.

No, no, no!

The baked custard, which was supposed to be smooth as silk, was speckled and lumpy. Like badly scrambled eggs.

The lasagne was worse.

How could this have happened?

The lasagne had been a work of art when it went into the oven—a symphony of layers—creamy yellow cheese sauce and pasta, with red tomatoes and herb infused meat.

Now the cheese sauce had mysteriously disappeared and the beautiful layers were dried out and brown, like shrivelled, knobbly cardboard splattered with dubious blobs of desiccated meat.

It was a total, unmitigated disaster.

'I can't believe it,' she whispered, crestfallen. She'd spent hours and hours preparing these dishes—beating, stirring, spicing, testing, reading and rereading the recipes over and over.

'What's happened?' Will's question was tentative, careful.

Fighting tears, Lucy shook her head. 'I don't know. I followed the instructions to the letter.' Snatching up oven gloves, she took out the heavy lasagne pan.

Stupidly, she'd been picturing Will's admiration. 'It's disgusting,' she wailed.

'It'll probably taste fine,' he said gallantly as she dumped the hot dish onto a table mat.

Lucy wanted to howl. 'I'm sorry, Will.' Unwilling to meet his gaze, she retrieved the dreadful looking custard and set it out of sight on the bench, beneath a tea towel. 'They've opened a pizza place in town. I think I'd better run in there.'

'This food will be fine,' he insisted again.

Hands on hips, she shook her head and glared at the stove. 'I can't believe I spent so much money on a brand-new oven and I still made a hash of the meal.'

'It might be a matter of getting used to the settings.' He bent closer to look at the stove's knobs.

Lucy followed his gaze and squinted at the little symbols. Now that she took a closer look, she saw that a tiny wriggly line on one knob differentiated it from its neighbour.

She swore softly. 'I think I turned the wrong knob. Damn! I've been trying to grill the food instead of baking it.'

She'd been too distracted. That was her problem. She'd kept thinking about the *reason* for this dinner and a moment's loss of concentration was all it had taken to ruin her efforts.

Will's grey eyes twinkled, however, and he looked as if he was trying very hard not to laugh.

To Lucy's surprise, she began to giggle. She'd been so tense about this evening, so desperate for everything to be perfect and now, when she had to try to cover her disappointment, she could only giggle.

It was that or cry, and she wasn't going to cry.

Will flung his arm around her shoulders in a friendly cheer-up hug, and her giggling stopped as if he'd turned off a switch.

'Right,' she said breathlessly as she struggled for composure. 'If we're going to try to eat this, I'd better set the table.'

Will opened a long-necked bottle with a fancy label and poured dark ruby-red wine into their glasses. Lucy took the salad she'd prepared from the fridge. At least it still looked fresh and crisp. She removed the plastic film, added dressing and tossed it. She found a large knife and cut the lasagne and was surprised that it cut easily, neatly keeping its shape. That was something, at any rate.

'I told you this would taste good,' Will said after his first mouthful.

To Lucy's surprise, he was right. The lasagne's texture might have been a bit too dry, but it hadn't actually burned and the herbs and meat had blended into a tasty combination. She sipped the deep rich wine and ate a little more and she began to relax. Just a little.

'Have you rescued any more pythons?'

She shook her head. 'The only wildlife I've cared for this week is a galah with a broken wing. But I discovered who dropped the python off. It was one of the schoolteachers. Apparently, he accidentally clipped him with his ride-on mower. He's going to care for him for another week or so, then let him go again in the trees down near the creek.'

They talked a little more about Lucy's work, including the good news that the footrot hadn't spread to any more sheep farms.

'What have you been up to?' she asked. 'I hear you've been lending a hand with drenching.'

He sent her a wry smile. 'News travels fast.'

'I saw your father in town the other day and he was so excited. He said you haven't lost the knack.'

Will shrugged.

'I told you you're a natural with animals.'

'Are you trying to turn me into a farmer, too?'

She didn't want to upset him, so she tried another topic. 'Have you started job-hunting?'

Over the rim of his wine glass his eyes regarded her steadily, almost with a challenge. 'I'm going for an interview at Armidale University next Thursday.'

Lucy could feel her smile straining at the edges, which was ridiculous. She knew Will would never settle back in the Willow Creek district. 'That's great. Good luck.'

'Thanks.'

He helped himself to seconds, but Lucy was too tense to eat any more and she wasn't sure if she should offer Will the dessert. However, he insisted on trying her lumpy custard and rum-poached pineapple and he assured her it was fabulous.

'Very courteous of you to say so.' She took a small spoonful of the custard. 'Actually, this does have a scrumptious flavour, doesn't it?' She smiled ruefully. 'At least I had all the right ingredients.'

'And that's what counts.'

Something about the way Will said this made Lucy wonder if he was talking about more than the food. With a rush of heat, she remembered again what this night was all about.

The butterflies in her stomach went crazy as she stared at the mouthful of wine in the bottom of her glass. In a perfect world, people created babies out of love, but tonight she and Will were supposed to make a baby by having 'friendly' sex.

Leave your emotions at the door, please.

She wasn't sure this was possible for her. But, if she wanted a baby, she was going to have to pretend that she was OK about the 'only friends' part of their arrangement.

Cicadas started their deafening chorus outside in the trees and in the soft pink-plumed grasses, as they did every evening in spring and summer, calling to each other in the last of the daylight.

Lucy cocked her ear to the almost deafening choir outside. 'Those cicadas are just like us.'

Will's eyebrows lifted. 'They are?'

'Sure. Listen to them. They wait till the last ten or fifteen minutes of daylight, till it's almost too late to find partners, and then they go into a mad panic and start yelling out—*Hey, I need to pass on my DNA. I need a mate. Who's out there?*'

Will laughed and topped up their wine glasses.

A startling image jumped into her head of his white shirt slipping from his broad brown shoulders, of the fastener on his jeans sliding down.

Consumed by flames, she gulped too much wine. 'This would be so much easier if we were aliens.'

Will almost choked on his drink. 'I beg your pardon?'

'Oh, you've seen the movies.' She held out her hand to him, fingers splayed. 'If aliens want to have a baby, they just let their fingertips touch. Or they hook up by mental telepathy and *voila*! One cute triangular baby.'

Shaking his head, Will stood. He wasn't smiling any more as he collected their plates and took them to the sink.

Slightly dazed by this abrupt change, Lucy watched him with a mixture of nervousness and longing. His long legs and wide shoulders—*everything*, really—made him so hunky and desirable.

'Shall I put the leftovers in the fridge?' he asked.

Goodness. He was hunky and desirable and unafraid to help in the kitchen. Lucy was so busy admiring Will she almost forgot that this was her kitchen and she should be helping him.

She jumped to her feet. 'My dogs will adore that custard in the morning.'

They made short work of clearing the food away, then Will snagged the wine bottle and their glasses. 'Why don't we make ourselves more comfortable?'

'C-comfortable?'

He smiled at her. 'If you stay here chattering about mating cicadas and alien sex you're going to talk yourself out of this, Goose.'

Well, yes, she was aware of that distinct possibility.

'Where do you want to go, then?'

Amusement shimmered in his eyes. 'I thought we might try your bedroom.'

Lucy gasped. 'Already?'

'Come on.' Will was smiling again as he took her hand. 'We can do this.' He pulled her gently but purposefully across the room. 'Which way?'

'My room's the first on the right.' Lucy was super-aware of their linked hands as she walked beside him on unsteady legs.

Think about the baby. Don't fall in love.

Will stopped just inside her bedroom doorway. 'Very nice,' he said, admiring the brand-new claret duvet with silvery-grey pillows. She'd chosen the pillow slips because they were the colour of Will's eyes.

She was glad she'd turned on the bed lamps and drawn the new curtains. The room looked welcoming. Not too girly. Smart. Attractive.

Will put the bottle and glasses down on one of the bedside tables, then came and stood beside her. He took her hands.

Lucy's mouth was drier than the Sahara. How could he be so calm?

She felt a riff of panic, found herself staring at his shoes, thinking about them coming off and then the rest of him becoming bare. She could picture his shoulders, his chest, his tapering torso…

He was so gorgeous, but he was only doing this because he wanted to help her. He only thought of her as a friend. He couldn't possibly fancy her. She'd always known that.

If she'd ever doubted it, she only had to remember the way Will had kissed her on the night of his farewell party, and then left for overseas as if it hadn't meant a thing. Now he would be so much more experienced with women.

Oh, help. It was ages since she'd had a boyfriend. Why had she agreed to this? How had she ever thought this could be OK?

'Will, I don't think—'

'That's good.'

'Pardon?'

'Don't think,' he murmured and he smiled as he drew her closer.

Nervously, she looked down at their linked hands and watched his thumb gently rub her knuckles. She wondered if she should warn him she was scared—scared of not living up to his expectations. Scared of falling in love.

But no. He was so confident and calm about this, he probably wouldn't understand. She could frighten him off and she would end up without a baby.

'I want our baby to be like you,' Will said softly.

Lucy gulped. 'Do you? Why?'

'You're so sweet, so clever and kind.'

'You're all of those things too.'

She saw the stirring of something dark and dangerous in his eyes.

He touched her collarbone and she held her breath as his fingers traced its straight line. Her pulses leapt as he reached the base of her throat.

'Any baby who scores you as his mum will be born lucky.' His voice was a deep, warm rumble running over her skin like a fiery caress.

She could see Will's mouth in the lamplight. So incredibly near. She remembered that one time he'd kissed her and how she'd marvelled that his lips were surprisingly soft and sensuous compared with the rough and grainy texture of his jaw.

He trailed his fingers up the line of her throat to her chin and, for a hushed moment, his thumb rode the rounded nub, then continued along the delicate edge of her jaw.

She held her breath as he lowered his head, letting his lips follow where his fingers had led.

Despite her tension, a soft sigh floated from her and she closed her eyes as his breath feathered over her skin and she felt the warm, intimate pressure of his mouth on the hollow at the base of her throat.

He was unbelievably good at this. Her tension began to melt beneath the sweet, intoxicating journey of his lips over her throat.

He whispered her name.

'Lucy.'

His lips caressed her jaw with whisper-soft kisses. He kissed her cheek, giving the corner of her mouth the tiniest lick, and she began to tremble.

Please, Will, please...

At last his lips settled over hers and Lucy forgot to be frightened.

Her lips parted beneath him and he immediately took the kiss deeper, tasting her fully, and she decided it was too late to worry about what Will thought of her. About having babies or not having them. She just wanted to enjoy this moment.

This, now.

Will framed her face with his hands and he kissed her eagerly, ardently, hungrily and Lucy returned his kisses, shyly at first but with growing enthusiasm, eager to relearn the wonderful texture and taste of him.

His voice was ragged and breathless as he fingered the straps of her dress. 'How do I get you out of this?'

'Oh, gosh, I forgot. Sorry.' The spell was broken as Lucy remembered that her dress had a side zipper. She had to lift one arm as she reached for it.

'I've got it,' Will said, his fingers beating hers to the task.

She heard the zip sliding south, felt his hands tweak her shoulder straps and suddenly her dress was drifting soundlessly to her feet. She wasn't wearing a bra and she felt vulnerable and shy, but Will drew her close, enfolding her into a comforting embrace.

With his arms around her, with his forehead pressed to hers, he whispered, 'Your turn, Goose.'

'My turn?'

'Take off my shirt.'

'Oh, yes. Right.'

Her eyes were riveted on his chest as she undid the buttons to reveal smooth masculine muscles that she longed to touch. She felt breathless and dizzy as she slid the fabric from his shoulders.

Her breath caught at the sight of him. She'd known he was beautiful, but she'd forgotten he was *this* beautiful.

Will kissed her again, letting his lips roam over hers in slow, lazy caresses that made her dreamy and warm so that again she gave up being scared. Still kissing her, he drew her down to the edge of the bed and then he took her with him until they were lying together, their limbs and bodies touching, meshing, already finding the perfect fit.

Bravely, she allowed her fingers to trail over his chest and felt his heart pounding beneath her touch. She smelled the long remembered midnight scent of his skin and she closed her eyes and gave in to sensation as he kissed her ears, her throat, her shoulder.

Every touch, every brush of his lips on her skin, every touch felt right and perfect and necessary.

She wasn't sure when she first felt the hot tears on her face, but she smiled, knowing they were tears of happiness.

How could they be anything else? This was her man, her passionate, hunky Will, and she was finally awake in her dream.

CHAPTER SEVEN

They sat in a pool of soft golden lamplight.

Will moved to the edge of the bed, shaken by what had happened.

He'd known that making love to Lucy would be a sweet pleasure, but he hadn't expected to be sent flying to the outer limits of the universe.

He felt an urge to ask her: *Does this change…everything*?

But that was lovers' talk and she expected friendship from him. Nothing more.

His thoughts churned while Lucy lay very still, with her knees bent and her shoulders propped against the pillows. She looked deceptively angelic with her short golden curls and a white sheet pulled demurely up to her chin.

'I mustn't move,' she said.

'Why can't you move?'

'I want to give your swimmers their very best chance of reaching my egg.'

He smiled at the hopeful light in her blue eyes, but his smile felt frayed around the edges.

It was hard to believe that this folly had been his idea. His foolish idea.

Lucy had been joking when she'd first suggested this, but he'd turned it into something real. He'd thought he was so damned clever. But he hadn't known, had he? Hadn't dreamed that making love to Lucy would turn his world upside down.

Was this how it had been for Josh?

He forced himself to remember why they'd done this. 'So I guess it's now a matter of wait and see?' he asked.

Lucy nodded. 'My period's due in about two weeks.'

So matter of fact.

Two weeks felt like a lifetime. 'I'll wait for another phone call then,' he said. 'And I'll hope for good news.'

Her eyes shimmered damply. Shyly, she said, 'Thank you, Will.'

His abrupt laugh was closer to a cough.

A tear sparkled and fell onto Lucy's flushed cheek, making him think of a raindrop on a rose. Reaching out, he gently blotted the shining moisture with the pad of his thumb. 'You OK, Goose?'

'Sure.'

She smiled to prove it and he launched to his feet and dragged on jeans. 'Can I make you a cup of tea or something?'

Lucy looked startled.

'I just thought…' He scratched at his bare chest. 'If you're planning to lie there for a bit, I thought you might like a cuppa.'

'Oh…um…well, yes, that would be lovely. Thank you.'

He went through to her kitchen, filled the kettle, set it on the stove and, as he rattled about searching for teabags and mugs, he saw a familiar piece of framed glass hanging in the window.

It was dark outside so he couldn't see the jewel-bright

colours of the stained glass, but he knew the dominant colour was deep blue.

Memories unravelled. He'd given this to Lucy as a graduation gift, to remind her of the times they'd spent as schoolkids fossicking for sapphires.

She'd always been fascinated by the change in the chips of dark sapphire when they were held up to the light and transformed from dull black into sparkling, brilliant blue.

The same thing happened when sun lit the stained glass.

But he hadn't expected her to keep this gift for so long, or to display it so prominently, as if it was important.

Now, Will looked around, trying to guess which piece among Lucy's knick-knacks had been a present to her from his brother.

Lucy managed not to cry until after Will had left. She heard the front door open and close, heard his footsteps on the front path, the rusty squeak of the front gate, the even rustier squeak of the truck's door and then, at last, the throaty grumble of the motor.

As the truck rattled away from her house, she couldn't hold back any longer.

The mug of tea Will had made for her sat untouched on the bedside table, and the tears streamed down her face.

She should have known.

She should have known this was a terrible mistake. Should have known Will Carruthers would break her heart.

Her sobs grew louder and she pulled a pillow against her mouth to muffle them, but nothing could diminish the storm inside her.

She loved Will. Loved him, loved him, loved him, loved him.

She'd always loved Will, and she'd wrecked her whole life by getting involved with his brother in a bid to make him jealous. She felt so guilty about that. And even now her memories of her mistakes cast a shadow over what had happened tonight.

Almost two weeks later, Lucy bought a packet of liquorice allsorts.

It was an impulse purchase in the middle of her weekly shopping. She saw the sweets, felt the urge to buy them and tossed them into her supermarket trolley. It wasn't until she was unpacking her groceries at home that she realised what she'd done and what it meant.

She only ever had the urge to eat sweets on the day before her period was due.

Which meant…

No.

No, no, no.

This didn't mean she wasn't pregnant, surely?

She'd been tense all week, alert to the tiniest signs in her body. But she hadn't noticed any of the well-known symptoms. No unusual tiredness. No breast tenderness. And now—she was having pre-menstrual cravings!

She couldn't bear it if her period came. She so wanted to be pregnant.

Just this week she'd delivered five Dachshund puppies and two purebred Persian kittens and each time she'd handled a gorgeous newborn she'd imagined her own little baby already forming inside her.

Heavens, she'd imagined her entire pregnancy in vivid detail. She'd even pictured the baby's birth and Will's excitement. She'd pictured bringing the little one home, watching it grow until it was old enough to play with Gina and Tom's twins. She'd almost gone into Willowbank's one and only baby store and bought a tiny set of clothes.

She *had* to be pregnant.

But now, on a rainy Friday night, she sat curled in a lounge chair with the bag of liquorice in her lap, aware of a telltale ache in her lower abdomen.

She was trying to stay positive. And failing miserably.

She'd had so much hope pinned on this one chance. She couldn't risk another night in bed with Will, couldn't go through another round of heartache. She really, really needed that one night to have been successful.

Time dragged for Will.

November, however, was a hectic month on a New South Wales sheep farm so, even though he couldn't stop thinking about Lucy, he found plenty of ways to keep busy.

Now that the shearing was over, all the sheep had to be dipped and drenched, prior to the long, hot summer. It was time to wean lambs and to purchase rams for next year's joining. To top it off, it was also haymaking time.

Will found himself slipping back into the world of his childhood with surprising ease.

In his wide-ranging travels, he'd seen breathtaking natural beauty and sights that were truly stranger than fiction, but it was only here at home that he felt a soul-deep connection to the land.

He supposed it flowed in his blood as certainly as his DNA. He'd always been secretly proud of the fact that his great great-grandfather, another William Carruthers, had bought this land in the nineteenth century.

William had camped here at first and then lived in the

shearers' quarters, before finally acquiring sufficient funds to build a substantial homestead for his bride.

Will found himself thinking more and more often about Josh, too. His brother had been the family member everyone had expected to work this land as their father's right hand man. The man who had won Lucy's heart.

He remembered the fateful morning Josh had woken him early, proclaiming that this was the day he was going to fly the plane he'd worked on for so long.

It had been too soon. Will had known that the final checks hadn't been made by the inspector from the aero club, but Josh had been insistent.

'I'm not waiting around for that old codger. I've put in all the work on this girl. I know she's fine. This is the day, Will. It's a perfect morning for a first flight. I can *feel* it.'

Will had gone with great reluctance, mainly to make sure Josh didn't do anything really stupid. As they drove through the creamy dawn towards the Willowbank airfield, he'd conscientiously reread all the flying manuals, anxious to understand all the necessary safety checks.

'I still don't think you should be doing this,' he'd said again when they'd arrived at the hangar.

'Give it a miss, little brother,' Josh had responded angrily. 'Just accept that we're different. I'm my own man. I go after what I want and I make sure that I get it.'

'Is that how you scored Lucy McKenty?' Will hadn't been able to hold back the question that had plagued him ever since he'd arrived home.

Josh laughed. 'Of course. What did you expect? In case you haven't noticed, Lucy's the best looking girl in the district. I wasn't going to leave her sitting on the shelf.'

'She's not another of your damn trophies.'

'For God's sake, Will, you're not going to be precious, are you?'

An unreasonable anger had swirled through Will. His
hands had fisted, wanting to smash the annoying smirk on
his brother's handsome face. 'You'd better make bloody
sure you look after her.'

'Don't worry.' Josh laughed. 'I've already done that.' He
was still laughing as he climbed into the pilot's seat. 'Now,
you sit over there and stay quiet, little brother, while I take
this little beauty for her test flight.'

Once more, Will had tried to stop him. 'You shouldn't be
doing this. You only have to wait for one more inspection.'

Josh had ignored him and turned on the engine.

'I'm not going to sit around here like your fan club,' Will
shouted above the engine's roar. 'If you're going to break
your bloody neck, you can do it by yourself.'

From the cockpit, Josh had yelled his last order. 'Don't
you dare take the car.'

'Don't worry. I'll bloody walk back.'

They had been his parting words.

The plane had barely made it into the air before it had
shuddered and begun to fall. Will had seen everything
from the road.

So many times in the years that followed, he'd regretted his actions that morning.

He'd washed his hands of his brother, turned his back
on him, but he should have stood up to Josh, should have
found a way to stop him.

But then again, no one, not even their father had been
able to stop Josh when he'd set his mind on a goal.

Lucy wouldn't have stood a chance either.

* * *

The next morning, Lucy knew the worst.

She sent Will a text message.

Thanks for your help, but sorry, no luck. We're not going to be parents. L x

She felt guilty about texting him rather than speaking to him, but she was afraid she'd start blubbing if she'd tried explain over the phone.

If Will's parents were nearby when he took the call, it would be really awkward for him to have to deal with a crying female who wasn't actually his girlfriend.

But it was a Saturday morning and she wasn't working, so she wasn't totally surprised when Will turned up on her doorstep within twenty minutes.

She hadn't seen him in two weeks and when she opened her door and saw him standing there with his heart-throb smile and blue jeans sexiness she felt a sweet, shivery ache from her breastbone to her toes.

'I guess you got my text,' she said.

Will nodded. 'I'm really sorry about your news, Lucy. It's rotten luck.'

She quickly bit her lower lip to stop it from trembling and, somehow, she refrained from flinging her arms around Will and sobbing all over him, even though it was exactly what she needed to do.

Instead she took two hasty steps back, tried for an offhand shrug. 'I guess it wasn't meant to happen.'

Will shook his head. 'I can't believe that.'

Her attempt to smile felt exceptionally shaky.

As they went through to the kitchen, she couldn't help remembering the last time they had been here together on *that* night.

'I should warn you, Will, I'm rather fragile this morning.'

Her hands fluttered in a gesture of helplessness. 'Hormones and disappointment can be a messy combination.'

'Maybe we were expecting too much, hoping it would all happen the first time.'

'I don't know. Maybe I should have more tests. I'm so scared that my eggs aren't up to scratch.'

Before she knew quite what was happening, Will closed the gap between them. His arms were around her and she was clinging to him, snuffling against his clean cotton T-shirt and inhaling the scents of the outdoors that clung to his skin. Trying very, very hard not to cry.

His fingers gently played with her hair. 'I'm sure your eggs are perfect. I bet they're the healthiest, cutest little goose eggs ever.'

She muffled a sob against his chest.

'We might have to be patient,' he said.

'Patient?' She pulled away. 'What do you mean?'

His eyes reflected bemusement. 'In a couple of weeks we can try again, can't we?'

No. No, they couldn't. She couldn't do this again. It had been a mistake.

'No, Will.' Lucy swallowed. 'I'm afraid we can't try again.'

Unhappily she slipped from the haven of his arms and turned away from the puzzled look in his eyes.

'But surely you're not ready to give up after just one try?'

'Yes, I am. Perhaps nature knows best.'

'What are you talking about?'

'Perhaps friends shouldn't try to be parents.'

'Lucy, that's not rational.'

'I'm sorry if you're disappointed, but I couldn't go through this again.'

Not with Will. It would be a huge mistake to sleep with

him again. It was too painful, knowing that he was only being a friend to her, that he didn't love her.

In the agonising stretch of silence he stood with his arms folded, frowning at a spot on the floor. Eventually, he said, 'You're disappointed right now. That's understandable. But you're sure to feel differently in another week or so.'

Lucy shook her head. 'No, Will. I'm sorry. This isn't a snap decision I made this morning. I'd already made up my mind last week. I decided I should give up on the whole idea of a baby if there was no pregnancy this month.'

'But that doesn't make sense.'

Tears threatened, but she kept her expression carefully calm. 'It makes sense to me.'

If only she could explain her decision without confessing that she had always been in love with him. But that meant talking about Josh and she felt too fragile this morning to go there.

Perhaps it was better to never talk about it. If they stopped the friendship plan now, they could leave the past in the past, where it belonged.

Somehow she kept her voice steady. 'It was a great idea in theory, but I'm afraid it's not going to work, Will. I might take months to fall pregnant. *Friends* don't keep having sex month after month, or possibly several times a month, trying to becoming parents.'

'But I thought you really wanted to have a baby.'

'Well, yes, I did want a baby. But—' Oh, help. What could she tell him? 'Maybe sex is different for guys,' she finished lamely.

'I wouldn't be so sure about that.'

Lucy's heart stuttered as she watched a dark stain ride

up Will's neck. Knotted veins stood out on the backs of his hands as he gripped the back of a kitchen chair.

Lucy knew she mustn't cave in now. She should have recognised from the start that this convenient baby idea could never work. She should have known that her emotions would never survive the strain of making love to him when he'd only ever offered her friendship and a fly in, fly out version of fatherhood.

She should have heard the warning bells then. She'd been foolish to agree.

Even so, a huge part of her wanted to remain foolish. She longed to rush into Will's arms again. She longed for him to kiss her, longed for a future where Will Carruthers figured in her life, no matter how remotely.

'So,' he said tightly, 'you're quite certain you want to ditch our arrangement?'

'Yes, that's what I want.'

His jaw clenched tightly and a muscle jerked just below his right cheekbone. For a moment he looked as if he wanted to say more, but then he frowned and shook his head.

'Will, I do appreciate your—'

He silenced her with a raised hand. 'Please, spare me your thanks. I know what this is all about. It's OK.' Already he was heading back down the hallway to her front door.

Puzzled by his sudden acceptance, but aching with regret, Lucy followed. On the doorstep, she said, 'Gina's invited me to the twins' christening. I guess I'll…see you there?'

'Of course.' He smiled wryly, 'We're the star godparents.'

It occurred to Lucy that this christening would be like the wedding—another gathering of their friends and families. Another ceremonial rite of passage. Another occasion when she and Will would be in close proximity. But she wondered if either of them could look forward to it.

The heaviness inside her plunged deeper as she watched Will swing into the truck. It was only as the driver's door slammed shut that she remembered she hadn't asked him about his job interview.

She ran down the path, calling to him, 'Will, how was the interview in Armidale?'

His face was stony. 'I didn't end up going.'

Shocked, she clung to her rickety front gate. 'Why not?'

'When I really thought about working there, shut up in a building all day, preparing lectures, marking papers, talking to academics, I knew I wasn't cut out for it.'

Before she could respond, he gunned the truck's motor and sent it rattling and roaring to life. Without smiling, he raised his hand in a grim salute. Dust rose as he took off.

Miserably, Lucy watched him go.

Soon he would probably disappear completely, off to another remote outpost. Now, too late, she realised that she'd been secretly hoping he'd get that job in Armidale and stay close.

At least Will had been honest with himself. He was right—unfortunately—Armidale wouldn't have suited him. Alaska or Africa were more his style. Anywhere—as long as it was a long, long way from Willowbank.

The christening was perfect—sweet babies in white baptismal gowns, white candles, a kindly vicar, photos and happy onlookers.

But it was an ordeal for Will.

Lucy was a constant distraction in a floaty dress of the palest dove grey, and Gina and Tom's obvious pride in their beyond cute, well behaved babies was a poignant reminder of her recent disappointment.

Spring was at its best with clear blue skies and gentle sunshine, but Will felt like a man on a knife edge. He so regretted not being able to help Lucy to achieve her goal of motherhood.

He was deeply disappointed that she wasn't prepared to have a second try. In fact, the depth of his disappointment surprised him. It was disturbing to know that she'd found the whole process too stressful.

Will reasoned that his relationship to Josh was the problem. He was too strong a reminder of the man she'd loved and lost. Why else had she looked so miserable when he'd tried to convince her to keep trying?

After the church service, the Carruthers family held a celebratory luncheon at Tambaroora. Long tables were covered in white cloths and set beneath pergolas heavy with fragrant wisteria. Everyone helped to carry the food from the kitchen—platters of seafood and roast meat, four different kinds of salads, mountains of crispy, homemade bread rolls.

Two white christening cakes were given pride of place and crystal flutes were filled with French champagne to wet the babies' heads.

Will chatted with guests and helped with handing the drinks around and Lucy did the same but, apart from exchanging polite greetings, they managed to avoid conversing with each other.

It seemed necessary given the circumstances, as if they both feared that a conversation might give their strained relationship away.

Fortunately, no one else seemed to notice their tension.

Everyone was too taken with the babies, or too eager to hear about Mattie and Jake's honeymoon travels in Italy.

Gina's father-in-law, Fred Hutchins, broke off an animated conversation with Lucy to catch Will as he passed.

'Great to see you again,' Fred said, shaking Will's hand. 'We old-timers have been following your exploits in Alaska and Africa and Mongolia. It all sounds so exciting.'

'It's been interesting,' Will agreed, without meeting Lucy's gaze.

'Good for you. Why not enjoy an adventurous life while you can? I should have headed off myself when I was younger, but it just didn't happen. I'm pleased you didn't get bogged down here, Will. I suppose, in some ways, we look on you as the one who got away.' Fred chuckled. 'When are you heading off again?'

'Pretty soon.'

Fred clapped Will on the shoulder. 'Good for you, son. Don't hang around here. It's too easy to grow roots in a place like this.'

Will caught Lucy's eye and saw the sad set of her mouth and the thinness of her smile. He wondered, as the laughter and chatter floated about them, if he was the only one who noticed the shadowy wistfulness in her eyes whenever she glanced in the direction of the babies.

Unlike the other women, Lucy hadn't begged for a chance to cuddle little Mia or Jasper and Will's heart ached for her.

When it was time for dessert, silver platters piled with dainty lemon meringue tarts appeared.

'Lucy, these are divine!' Gina exclaimed with her mouth full.

For the first time that day, Lucy looked happy. 'They turned out well, didn't they?'

'Did you make these?' Will was unable to disguise his surprise, which he immediately regretted.

Lucy's smile faltered. 'Yes.' She tilted her chin defensively. 'As a matter of fact, I made them entirely from scratch—even the pastry.'

'What's got into you, Will?' Gina challenged. 'Are you trying to suggest that Lucy can't cook?'

The eyes of almost every guest at the table suddenly fixed on Will and he felt the back of his neck grow uncomfortably hot. He smiled, tried to mumble an apology. 'No, no, sorry. I...I...'

To his surprise, Lucy came to his rescue. 'Back when Will and I were at uni, I used to be an atrocious cook.'

This was greeted by indulgent smiles and nods and comments along the lines that Lucy was an accomplished cook now. As general conversation resumed, Lucy's eyes met Will's down the length of the table. She sent him a smile, nothing more than a brief flash, but its sweet intimacy almost undid him.

Shortly afterwards, the babies woke from their naps and the christening cakes were cut and glasses were raised once again. Tom made a short but touching speech of thanks to Mattie for her wonderful gift of the surrogate pregnancy and, just as he finished, baby Mia let out a loud bellow of protest.

'Oh, who's a grizzly grump?' Gina gave a theatrical groan. 'She probably needs changing.'

To Will's surprise, Lucy jumped to her feet and held out her arms. 'Let me look after her,' she said.

'Oh, thanks, I won't say no,' Gina replied with a laugh.

Lucy was smiling as she scooped the baby from Gina's lap. Will watched her walk back across the smooth lawn to the house and thought how beautiful she looked in her elegant dress with its floaty grey skirt, the colour of an early morning sky. Her pale blonde hair was shining in the sunlight, and the baby was a delicate pink and white bundle in her arms.

Without quite realising what he'd done or why, he found himself standing. 'I'll fetch more champagne,' he offered, grasping for an excuse to follow her.

'No need, Will,' called his father, pointing to a tub filled with ice. 'We still have plenty of champers here.'

'I…er…remembered that I left a couple of bottles in the freezer,' Will said. 'I don't want them to ice up. I'd better rescue them.'

As he entered the house he heard Lucy's voice drifting down the hallway from the room that used to be Gina's. Her voice rippled with laughter and she was talking in the lilting sing-song that adults always used with babies. For Will, the sound was as seriously seductive as a siren's song and he couldn't resist heading down the passage.

In the doorway he paused, unwilling to intrude. The baby was on the bed, little arms waving, legs pumping as she laughed and giggled and Lucy was leaning over her.

Will couldn't see Lucy's face, but he could hear her soft, playful chatter. It was such a touching and intimate exchange. A painful brick lodged in his throat.

Lucy was laughing. 'Who's the cutest little baby girl in the whole wide world?'

Mia responded with loud chuckles and coos.

'Who's the loveliest roly-poly girl? Who's so chubby and sweet I could gobble her up?'

Will felt a twist in his heart as he watched Lucy kiss the waving pink toes, watched her gently and deftly apply lotion to the petal soft skin, then refasten a clean nappy.

Aware that he was spying, he stepped back, preparing to make a discreet departure, but just at that moment, a choked cry broke from Lucy and she seemed to fold in the middle like a sapling lashed by a storm.

She sank to her knees beside the bed.

'Lucy.'

He didn't want to startle her, but her name burst from him.

Her head jerked up and she turned and her face was white and wet with tears. She looked at Will with haunted eyes and then she looked at the baby and she tried to swipe at her tears, but her emotions were too raw. Her mouth crumpled and she sent Will a look of hopeless despair.

In a heartbeat he was in the room, dropping to his knees beside her. He pulled her into his arms and he held her as she trembled and clung to him, burying her face, warm and wet with tears, against his neck.

It was then that he knew.

He knew how deeply she longed for a child.

He knew how very much he wanted to help her.

Most of all, he knew that Lucy's need was greater than her fear.

'We can try again if you like,' he whispered close to her ear. 'Lucy, why don't you try again?'

'Yes,' she sobbed against his shoulder. 'I think I have to. Please, yes.'

His arms tightened around her.

In a few minutes Lucy was calmer. She stood and went to the bathroom to wash her face while Will held Mia.

It was quite something the way his little niece snuggled into him, with her head tucked against his chest and one chubby starfish hand clutching at the fabric of his shirt.

Will tried to imagine a son or daughter of his own. A tiny person like this. Mia smelled amazing. She smelled… pink.

Yes, if pale pink was a fragrance, he was sure it would smell like this baby. Warm and fuzzy and incredibly appealing.

The baby was wearing the gold bracelet he'd bought for her christening—a little chain with a heart shaped locket— and it almost disappeared into the roly-poly folds of her wrist. Her skin was so soft. Peach soft.

No, softer than a peach.

Wow. No wonder fathers wanted to protect their daughters.

'Oh, gosh, Will, that baby really suits you,' Lucy said, almost smiling as she came back into the room.

'Not as well as she suits you.'

He handed the tiny bundle back to Lucy and she buried her nose in Mia's hair. 'I'd bottle this smell if I could.'

Turning, she checked her appearance in the mirror above the dressing table. 'I just need a minute to compose myself. It's a pity I don't have my make-up with me.'

To Will, Lucy looked absolutely fine just as she was, but he offered to fetch her handbag.

'No, it's OK,' she said. 'You'd better go back to the party. Gina will be wondering why we're taking so long.'

CHAPTER EIGHT

LUCY'S words were prophetic. Will had barely left before
Gina appeared at the bedroom door.

'Oh, there you are,' she said. 'I was wondering—' She
stopped and frowned. 'Is everything OK, Lucy?'

'Yes.' Lucy dropped a swift kiss on the baby's head.
'Mia's fine.'

But gosh, she couldn't quite believe that she'd actually
agreed to try again for a baby with Will.

'But what about you?' Gina asked. 'You look upset.'

Lucy tried to shrug this aside.

'You've been crying.' Gina came closer, her dark eyes
warm with concern.

It was too hard to pretend. Lucy tried to smile but her
mouth twisted out of shape.

'Lucy, you poor thing. What's the matter?'

'I'm just emerald green with jealousy, that's all.' She
looked down at Mia, curled in her arms and this time she
managed a rueful smile. 'I would so love to have a little
one like this for myself.'

'Oh.' Gina made a soft sound of sympathy. 'I know how
awful that longing can be. It just eats you up, doesn't it?'

That was the great thing about Gina. She wasn't just a good friend. She really understood. She'd been through years of painful endometriosis before her doctor had finally told her that she needed a hysterectomy. The news that she could never have children had broken her heart, but then Mattie had stepped in with her wonderful surrogacy offer.

Now, just as she had when they'd been school friends, Gina plopped down on her old bed and patted a space for Lucy, who obeyed without question. She was so totally in need of a girly heart-to-heart and where better than Gina's bedroom, still painted the terrible lavender and hot pink she'd chosen when she was fourteen?

'Are you thinking about tackling another round of IVF?' Gina asked.

Lucy shook her head and hastily weighed up the pros and cons of confiding in Will's sister. Quite quickly she decided it was necessary. Out of any of the women in her circle of friends, Gina would most understand her longing for a baby. And she also understood her history with Will.

'I'm trying for a baby, but not with IVF,' she said.

To Gina's credit, she didn't look too shocked, although she was understandably puzzled. 'So how's that work? You have a secret boyfriend?'

'Not exactly.' Lucy settled Mia's sleepy head more comfortably into the crook of her arm. 'Actually, Will's offered to help me out.'

This time, Gina did look shocked.

Momentarily.

'Will's helping you to have a baby?'

'Yes.'

'Wow!' Gina gasped. 'That's…that's…far out. You and

Will.' She gave an excited little squeal. 'Gosh, Lucy, that's wonderful.'

'Unconventional is probably the word most people would use.'

Gina frowned. 'Excuse me? I'm lost.'

'Friends don't usually plan to have a baby together.'

'Friends?'

'Yes. Will and I are still only friends. But he's quite keen to be a dad and he knows how I feel, so he wants to help me to have a baby. It's actually rather convenient.'

'Right.' Gina frowned as she digested this. Then she smiled. 'But friends often fall in love.'

Lucy felt bad, knowing she was about to watch Gina's happy smile disintegrate.

'Not this time,' she said. 'There's no chance.'

For a moment Gina seemed lost for words. She traced the pattern of pink and lavender patchwork squares on the bed quilt. 'I guess it must be awkward,' she mused, 'because you were engaged to Josh.'

Unwilling to dwell on that subject, Lucy tried to steer Gina's thoughts in a different direction. 'The thing is, Will's not a settling down kind of guy. You and I both know that. We've always known it.'

Gina pulled a face. 'Will's annoying like that, isn't he? I really love my brother but, I have to admit, he's always been a bit of an outsider in our family. Middle child syndrome, I guess.'

'I wouldn't know. I was an only child.'

'In our family, it was always about Josh, as the eldest son. He was the heir apparent. And I was the spoiled baby girl. Poor old Will was caught in the middle, neither one thing nor the other.'

Gina lowered her voice importantly. 'Even though I was the youngest, I could see how it was. Dad spoiled me rotten. Gosh, when I was little, he used to take me out on the tractor every night just to get me to sleep. I'd sit up there with my security blanket and my head in his lap, while he went round and round the paddock.'

'Lucky you,' Lucy said.

'And then Josh was always trailing after Dad like a faithful sheepdog and the old man adored it. They were always together, working with the sheep, tinkering with machinery. They had a special bond and I'm sure Will felt left out. I think that's why he drifted towards books and study, rather than helping out on the farm. And then he started taking off on his own to fossick for rocks.'

'Which he's still doing, more or less,' Lucy suggested.

'I guess.' Gina let out a loud sigh. 'It's not fair on you, though.' She pulled at a loose thread in the quilt. 'Will might still feel as if he's living in Josh's shadow.'

Bright heat flared in Lucy's face. 'I hope he doesn't,' she said quietly.

'What is it with my brothers? Why do they both have to mess up your life?'

'Because I let them?'

Gina's face softened and she reached out to touch her daughter's hair as she slept in Lucy's arms. 'Well…for what it's worth, I think this baby idea is fabulous. OK, maybe it's a tad unconventional, but it's still fabulous. I do wish you luck.'

'Thanks.' Lucy smiled. It was good to know she had someone on her side. 'You won't say anything to Will?'

'Heavens, no.' Gina threw a reassuring arm around

Lucy's shoulders. 'A little sister's advice would be the kiss of death, and I really want this to work.'

After the last of the guests had left, Will helped with the dismantling of the trestle tables and the stacking away of the chairs in a storage room below the hayloft. As he worked, his thoughts were focused front, back and centre on Lucy.

It wasn't possible to think about anything else. His heart had cracked in two today when he'd seen her weeping beside little Mia.

Mattie had achieved the impossible for Gina and Tom and no doubt that made Lucy's situation all the more distressing. But what upset Will was the fact that she'd told him last week she wanted to call off their plan, when it was so obvious that she still wanted a baby.

There could only be one reason, of course. She wasn't happy about having to sleep with him again. He'd created a problem for her.

For possibly the thousandth time Will thought about that night. He'd been a lost man the minute he'd touched Lucy McKenty. That was his problem. One caress of her skin, one brush of his lips against her soft, sweet mouth and he'd forgotten his plan to have simple, 'friendly' sex with a focus on procreation. Damn it. He'd been so carried away, he'd practically forgotten his own name.

Problem was, he'd put their kiss of ten years ago out of his mind. He'd gone into this without thinking about how Lucy might taste, or how she'd react. He certainly hadn't expected such a passionate response from her.

Was that how she'd been with Josh?

Hell.

Will was shocked by the violent force of his feelings when he thought about Josh and Lucy together.

He tried to stop thinking about them but, with the last chair stacked, he strode to the end of the home paddock. He looked out across the valley to where the distant hills were blue smudges on the horizon and he drew a deep breath and caught the sharp tang of eucalyptus and the dusty scent of the earth.

He looked up at the wide faded blue of the sky, searching for answers to the turmoil inside him.

Some answers were easy. He knew exactly why Lucy loved this land, and he knew that he wanted his child to live here with her.

It felt right that Lucy should be the mother of his child. It felt good.

But was he fooling himself? Was it madness to think he could replace his brother?

No, he decided. It was actually a greater madness to dwell on the Josh-Lucy scenario, to keep letting the past haunt him.

For more than twenty years he'd lived in Josh's shadow, but it was time to get over that. His task now was to concentrate on the living. To do the right thing by Lucy.

Heaven knew she deserved to be treated well. She was a wonderful girl. Gutsy and clever. Sweet and fun.

She was his friend.

And she needed his help.

And he needed—

Hell, he wasn't sure what he needed from Lucy. He had the feeling though, that he couldn't stop wanting to help her.

But, if that was so, if they were going to keep trying until

Lucy was pregnant, he had to make this baby plan easier for her. Which meant he had to make sure that their next rendezvous was as friendly and functional as possible.

Will let out a sigh—which he smartly decided was a sigh of relief. He felt marginally better now that he had his thoughts straight.

All he had to remember was that he was Lucy's friend, not her lover.

Friendship gave them clear boundaries and boundaries were good. Breaking the boundaries could completely mess up her life.

In line with that thinking, he should start making plans to get a job outside this district. That way Lucy would know he wasn't going to crowd her once their goal of pregnancy was achieved. He'd heard of jobs in Papua New Guinea that he could apply for.

PNG wasn't too far away, so he could come back to Willowbank from time to time to play whatever role in their baby's life that Lucy wanted.

Good. Will was glad he had that sorted.

It always helped to have a plan.

Three days later he received a text message from Lucy:

Can you come over tonight? I have evening surgery, so can't offer dinner. Is 9.30 too late? L x

He sent a hasty reply:

I'll be there.

I'll be there…

All day Will's message drummed inside Lucy with a pulsing, electrifying beat.

She knew she was weak. She was supposed to be giving up on this baby idea and protecting her emotions, but she'd only spent five minutes with little Mia and her brave plans to abandon the project had toppled like bowling pins.

She shouldn't have jumped at Will's offer to try again for a baby, but heavens, if he hadn't offered, she might have begged him.

Now, she couldn't stop thinking about him arriving on her doorstep tonight, coming into her house, into her bed.

For the first time in her professional life she found it hard to concentrate on her work. She was excessively grateful that the tasks were routine, so she could more or less function on autopilot.

But, by the time the hands of the clock eventually crawled to nine-thirty in the evening, she was jangling with tension and expectation.

And she was falling apart with insecurity.

She wished she knew how Will really felt about this second night, but it was such a difficult question to broach. And she might not like his answer.

She told herself that she should be grateful he was willing to help, and she should be pleased that he hadn't pressed her to talk about Josh. If she started down that track, she might reveal too much about her feelings for Will. She could complicate the delicate balance of their friendship. Spoil everything.

Perhaps Will was nervous too, because he arrived two minutes and thirty-five seconds early, but Lucy opened the door even before he knocked.

'Evening, Lucy.' His smile was shy, yet so charming, she was sure it was designed to make her heart do back-flips.

She ran her damp hands down the side seams of her jeans. 'Come on in.'

Will came through the doorway but then he stopped abruptly. 'I've brought you a little something,' he said, holding out a slim box tied with curling purple ribbons.

'Oh.' Lucy gulped with surprise. 'Thank you.'

'I know rocks don't really have special powers, but see what you think.'

Her hands were shaking and she fumbled as she tried to undo the ribbon, pulling the knot tighter, instead of undoing it.

'Hey, I'll get that.'

The brush of Will's hands against hers sent rivers of heat up her arms. Her heart thumped as she watched the concentration in his face, the patience of his fingers as he deftly prised the knot free. Finally, he lifted the lid and showed her a neat little pendant on a pretty silver chain.

'Will, it's gorgeous. Is it an amethyst?'

'Yes.' He sent her another shy smile. 'Apparently, amethysts have traditionally been linked to fertility.'

'Oh, wow. That's so thoughtful. Thank you. It's beautiful. I love it.'

He smiled gorgeously. 'Let me do up the clasp for you.'

Lucy decided it was quite possible to melt just from being touched. She was burning up as Will fastened the pendant. She turned to him.

'It suits you,' he said. 'It brings out the deep blue in your eyes.'

To Lucy's surprise he looked suddenly nervous. Bravely, she stepped forward and kissed him. On the mouth.

Gosh. When had she become so brave?

Will returned her kiss carefully, almost chastely, and she felt a cold little swoop of disappointment.

She lifted her hands to his shoulders and felt him tense all over. 'Will,' she whispered, 'what's wrong?'

CHAPTER NINE

WILL knew he could do this.

All day, he'd rehearsed in his mind how he would make love to Lucy as her friend. He'd thought about nothing else as he'd driven the tractor up and down the paddocks at Tambaroora and the whole idea had seemed solid and plausible.

Now, however, Lucy was close—kissing close—and his certainty evaporated.

Or, rather, his certainty shifted focus. And the focus was *not* on friendship. Far from it.

He wanted nothing more than to gather Lucy in to him, to kiss her with the reckless frenzy of a lover, to kiss her slowly, all night long, to lose himself in her fragrant softness.

He wanted to forget *why* they were doing this. He wanted to forget her past history with his brother. He wanted to think of nothing but...

Lucy.

He wanted *her*.

Tonight.

She was simply dressed in jeans and a tomboyish grey T-shirt. No pretty floral dress. No sexy high heels.

It didn't matter. She was Lucy. And he wanted her.

Too much.

Her disappointment was clear as she stepped away from him and nervously fingered the amethyst, feeling the smooth facets beneath her fingertips. Her blue eyes were cloudy. Understandably perplexed. 'Will, there's something wrong, isn't there?'

'No,' he muttered and he forced his thoughts to focus on restraint.

'You don't want to…' she began, but she couldn't finish the sentence.

'I don't want to hurt you, Lucy.'

Cringe. Had he really said that? The only way he could hurt Lucy was by walking away and denying her the chance to become a mother.

Or perhaps that was the only way he could save himself from eternal damnation? Why the hell hadn't they stuck to the IVF option?

His throat worked.

Lucy looked away. They were still standing in her hallway, for heaven's sake.

'Would you like a drink?' she asked.

'A drink?' he repeated like a fool.

'To…er…relax.'

He shook his head. He would need a whole bottle of alcohol to douse the fire inside him.

Lucy looked as if she wanted to weep and he knew that, at any minute now, she would thank him for the gift and send him home. It was exactly what he deserved.

She dropped her gaze to the empty box in her hands. 'I thought a drink might help with…um…getting in the mood.'

With a choked sound that was halfway between a groan

and a sick laugh, Will fought back the urge to haul her against his hard, aroused body. 'There's nothing wrong with my mood, Lucy.'

'Right,' she whispered hoarsely, but she looked upset, a little shocked. And maybe just a tad angry. Her chin lifted and her unsmiling eyes confronted him.

His heart slammed inside his chest. He couldn't believe he'd been so cool about this last time. What a poor naïve fool he'd been. Back then, he hadn't known what it was like to take Lucy into his arms. He'd forgotten how dangerous it could be to get close to her, to know that the slim curves pressed so deliciously against him were Lucy's.

Until then, he'd innocently assumed that their kiss on the veranda all those years ago had been an aberration.

Now, Will knew better.

Now, he knew that kissing Lucy, making love to Lucy could all too easily become a dangerous addiction.

With a soft sigh, she set the box and purple ribbon on the hallstand, and when she looked at him again, she set her hands on her hips and her eyes were an unsettling blue challenge. 'What do you want to do, then?'

'Kiss you.'

The answer jumped from Will's lips before he could gather his wits. He saw the flare of confusion in Lucy's eyes, the soft surprised O of her mouth. But his hands were already reaching out for her and then he kissed her as if this were his last minute on this earth.

He kissed her as if at any moment he might lose her.

For ever.

Lucy couldn't quite believe this.

She hadn't dared to hope that Will could possibly want her with such intensity.

One minute he'd looked as if he wanted to bolt out her front door, the next his mouth was locked with hers. His hands cupped her bottom and he pulled her against him and suddenly she stopped worrying.

All the fantasies she'd lived through that day—actually, all the romantic fantasies she'd dreamed about her entire adult life—rolled into one sensational here and now.

Never had she experienced such a hot kiss. Flashpoints exploded all over her skin. Recklessly, she pushed even closer to Will, winding her arms around his neck, seeking the closest possible contact. To her relief, he most definitely didn't seem to mind.

Gosh, no.

His fever matched hers, kiss for kiss, and a kind of wonderful madness overcame them.

Together they made it down the hall, bumping against the walls in a frenzy of kissing and touching, until they reached the first doorway.

It led to the lounge room, and it seemed that would have to do.

They stumbled to the sofa, sinking needfully into its velvety cushions.

Bliss.

Bliss to help and be helped out of clothing. Bliss to lie together at last with Will, to run her hands over the satin of his skin as it stretched tightly over hard bands of muscle.

Even greater bliss when Will took charge and deliberately held back the pace, stilling her seeking hands and kissing her with unhurried, leisurely reverence.

It was sweet, so sweet. He kissed her slowly and deeply, drawing her gradually but relentlessly down into an intimate dark cave where only the two of them existed.

And everything was fine. It was perfect. Because this time she knew that Will Carruthers was the one man in the world she could trust to fulfil her innermost secret longings.

Will woke as the pale buttery light of dawn filtered though the curtains in Lucy's bedroom. He didn't move because she was still asleep with one arm flung across his chest and her soft, warm body nestled against him, her breath a sweet hush on his skin.

Staying with her till morning had not been part of his plan. Hell, practically none of last night had been part of his plan, although he had rationalised that he should make the most of this one night.

Tomorrow he was flying out to Papua New Guinea to check out job prospects.

At that thought Will suppressed a sigh, but perhaps Lucy felt it for she stirred against him and her blue eyes opened.

'Morning, Goose.' He thought about kissing her, but decided against it. This morning was all about seriously backing off.

Lucy looked at her bedside clock and groaned. 'I've slept in.'

He thought guiltily about the amount of time he'd kept her awake.

'I'm going to have to hurry,' she grumbled, reaching for a towelling robe draped over a nearby chair.

Will swung his legs over the edge of the bed.

Lucy tightened the knot at her waist and stood. She ran a hand through her tumbled curls and sent him an uncertain smile. She let her gaze travel over him, and it seemed to settle rather sadly on his bare feet.

He looked down. 'Yeah…I worry about that too.'

'What?'

'Whether the baby will inherit my freakishly long second toes.'

'Oh.' She laughed. 'It might end up with my freakishly tiny ears.'

He fought back an urge to pull her to him, to nibble and taste those neat little ears. 'Cutest ears in the southern hemisphere,' he said.

'But they might not look too flash on a boy.'

She bit her lower lip and touched the pendant at her throat. 'I wonder if it's happening, Will. I wonder if I'm pregnant.'

'You're sure to be,' he said and he did the only thing that was right.

He reached for his clothes.

Lucy held back her tears until after Will left, but she'd never felt so desolate. To watch him walk away was like cutting off a lifeline and she felt like an astronaut, adrift in endless emptiness.

But there was no point in letting him see how much she'd hated to let him go. He was heading off to Papua New Guinea tomorrow and he was sure to get a job there. She'd always known he was never going to be tamed and kept in one place.

He was a catch and release kind of man, like the wild bush creatures she cared for and then set free.

Will telephoned when he got back a week later. 'Have you started tucking into the liquorice allsorts?'

Lucy was relieved to report; 'Not yet.'

'Any symptoms?' he asked hopefully.

'Hard to say. It's still too soon, but I've been rather tired and I need to go to the bathroom in the middle of the night.'

'They're promising signs, aren't they?'

'Could be.'

Problem was, Lucy had become hyper-aware of her body, anxious to discover the slightest hint of change. She was sure she felt different this month, but she couldn't be certain that the differences were real and not simply the result of her overactive imagination.

Just in time she bit back an impulse to tell Will she'd missed him. But it was true, of course. She'd missed Will terribly. Desperately. The longer he'd stayed away the more she was certain that making love to him on a second night had been even more dangerous than she'd feared. She loved him.

Still.

Always.

With all her heart.

She could no longer hide from the truth and she had no idea how she could go on pretending anything else.

But she had to accept that Will was never going to change, never going to settle down. He might be attracted to her, but he'd always been restless and he would always need to keep travelling, seeking new sights and challenges.

When she was younger, she'd known this, and she'd tried to protect herself by simply being his friend. Now she'd thrown caution to the wind and she had to accept that her love for him was a weakness she'd have to learn to adjust to and live with—the way other people adjusted to a disability.

'How was your trip to Papua New Guinea?' she asked, keeping her voice carefully light.

'Oh, there's plenty of work up there. I've had a couple of offers, so it's a matter of deciding which job to take.'

'That's great.' Good grief, she hoped she didn't sound as unhappy as she felt. 'A very fortunate position to be in.'

'No doubt about that,' Will agreed. 'So…about you. This week is the week of the big countdown, right?'

'Yes.' Lucy let out a sigh. 'I wish I didn't have to wait. I'm afraid I've become mildly obsessive. I've taken to reading my stars in every magazine I can find. I've even thought about going to see Sylvie.'

'Who's Sylvie?'

'The hairdresser in the main street. She tells fortunes as well as cutting hair, but I'm not quite desperate enough to trust her talents. I'm actually trying very hard to be sensible and philosophical.'

'Will you use a home pregnancy test?'

'Oh, yes. Definitely. I've a carton of tests ready and waiting, but I'm holding off till next Friday. If I try too soon, I might get a false reading and I don't think I could bear the disappointment.'

'Lucy, I want to be there.'

The sudden urgency in his voice made her heart jump.

'You want to be here when I do the test?'

'Yes. Is that OK?'

She pressed a hand against her thudding heart. She shouldn't be surprised. The baby would be as much Will's as it was hers, but somehow she hadn't expected this level of interest from him.

'It doesn't seem right that you should be all alone when you find out,' he said.

She couldn't deny it would be wonderful to share her news with Will. If it was good news they could celebrate, and if she was disappointed again he would be there to comfort her.

'You'd better come over first thing on Friday morning,' she said and her voice was decidedly shaky.

Friday morning produced an idyllic country dawn. As Will drove to Lucy's place, the paddocks, the trees and the sky looked as if they'd been spring cleaned for a special occasion, and the landscape had a gentle and dreamy quality as if he was viewing the scene through a soft focus lens. The air was balmy and light.

A pretty white fog filled the bowl of Willow Creek and he watched it drift from the dark cluster of trees like magician's smoke. He felt keyed up, excited, anxious, hopeful.

Torn.

He longed for good news, but in many ways he dreaded it. If Lucy was pregnant, he would have no choice but to take a back seat in her life.

He found that prospect unexpectedly depressing so he tried, instead, to enjoy the picture perfect scenery.

It shouldn't have been difficult. The road from Tambaroora wound past a small forest of pines, then over a low hill before it dipped to a rustic bridge where another arm of Willow Creek was bordered by yellow and purple wildflowers.

But he was still feeling edgy when he reached Lucy's place, even though her dogs rushed to the front gate to greet him with excited barks and madly wagging tails.

Lucy was dressed for work in a khaki shirt and trousers, but he could see the amethyst pendant sitting above the open V of her shirt collar.

Valiantly, he ignored the urge to pull her in for a kiss.

'How are you feeling?' he asked her.

'Totally nervous,' she admitted. 'I didn't sleep very well.'

'Neither did I.'

She looked surprised. 'I…I'm assuming you'll stay for breakfast? I've started sausages and tomatoes.'

'Thanks. They smell great.'

'And I've made a pot of tea. Why don't you help yourself while I…er…get this done? I can't stand the suspense.'

'Off you go,' he said, but as she turned to leave he snagged her hand. 'Hey, Goose.'

Her blue eyes shimmered. 'Yes?'

'Good luck.'

To his surprise she stepped closer and gave him a swift, sweet kiss on the jaw. The room seemed intolerably empty when she left.

Will poured tea into a blue pottery mug and walked with it to the window, saw the stained glass feature winking bright blue in the morning light and felt shocked by the tension that filled him.

For Lucy's sake he really wanted this test to be positive.

He wondered about that other time, eight years ago, when she'd discovered she was pregnant. Had she been ecstatically happy? Just as quickly he dismissed the question. There was little to be achieved now by reminding himself that he could only ever be a second best option after Josh.

It was time to be positive, to look forward to the future. A new generation, perhaps.

When he heard Lucy's footsteps he set his mug down, unhappily aware that she wasn't hurrying. She hadn't called out in excitement.

He turned, arms ready to comfort her, and his heart stood still in his chest as he prepared himself for disappointment.

He didn't want to put extra pressure on her, so he

summoned a smile and tried to look calm, as if the result really didn't matter either way.

Lucy came into the kitchen and he saw two bright spots of colour in her cheeks. Her eyes were huge and shiny with emotion.

She waved a plastic stick. 'There are two lines.'

'What does that mean?'

'It means—'

She looked as if she was going to cry. Will's throat tightened.

'We did it, Will.'

She didn't look happy.

'You mean—' He hardly dared to ask. 'You're pregnant?'

'Yes!'

He wasn't sure if she was going to laugh or cry.

'Congratulations,' he said and his voice was choked. 'You clever girl.'

Tears glistened in her eyes but at last she was smiling. And then she was grinning.

'Can you believe it, Will? I'm pregnant!' With a happy little cry she stumbled towards him and he opened his arms.

'Thank you,' she cried as she hugged him.

'Congratulations,' he said again.

'Congratulations to you, too. You're going to be a father.'

He grinned shakily.

A soft look of wonder came over her face as she touched the amethyst pendant, then pressed her hands to her stomach. 'I'm going to be a mother.'

'The best mother ever.'

'I don't give a hoot if it's a boy or a girl.'

'Not at all,' Will agreed, although he realised with something of a shock that he would love to have a son.

Happiness shone in Lucy's eyes as she looked around her kitchen, as if she was suddenly seeing it with new eyes. She grinned at the table that she'd set for breakfast, at the dogs' bowls on the floor near the door. 'Oh, gosh, Will, I'm pregnant!'

He laughed, but it felt inadequate.

'Thank you,' she said again, and her smile was so sweet he wanted to sweep her into his arms, to hold her and kiss her and murmur endearments, all of which were completely inappropriate now that they were reverting to friendship.

Lucy's mind, however, was on a more practical plane. She looked over at the stove. 'I've probably burned the sausages.'

'They're OK. I turned them down low.'

'Well done. Thanks.' She glanced at the clock and sighed. 'We'd better eat. I still have a day's work ahead of me.'

'That's something we need to talk about,' Will said. 'You need to look after yourself now.'

She frowned at him, then shrugged. 'We can talk while we eat.'

It felt strangely intimate to be having breakfast with Lucy—pottering about in the kitchen, buttering toast, finding Vegemite and marmalade.

When they were settled at the table Lucy looked at him across the seersucker tablecloth, her blue eyes wide and innocent. 'Now, what were you saying about my work?'

'You're going to need some kind of support now you're pregnant. You can't manage such a big workload on your own.'

'I have an assistant.'

'But she can't take on the tough jobs like delivering diffi-cult calves. And she's not qualified to operate. I don't like the thought of you standing for long hours over difficult surgery.'

'Are you going to get bossy already?'

'You had a miscarriage once before,' he reminded her gently. 'And you're quite a bit older now.'

'Thanks for bringing that to my attention.' Lucy's mouth was tight as she spread Vegemite on her toast. 'Isn't it a bit hypocritical of you to be worrying about my age and personal safety?'

'Hypocritical?'

Her eyes blazed. 'You're not exactly taking care of yourself.'

'How do you mean?'

'You're about to become a father. You barely escaped with your life from your last job and you told me you'd learned a big lesson. But now you're heading off to Papua New Guinea, where a mudslide wiped out an entire village last summer. And everyone knows how often planes crash in the highlands. The airstrips are the size of postage stamps and they're perched on the edge of massive deep ravines.'

'I'm not going to the highlands.' Will rearranged the salt and pepper shakers like pieces on a chessboard. 'And I'm not the one who's pregnant. Your safety is more important than mine.'

Lucy opened her mouth as if she was going to say something more, but apparently changed her mind. She shrugged. 'Actually, I'd already been planning to cut back on work if I became pregnant. I can use locums. I have quite a few city vet friends who love it out here.'

'What kind of friends?' Will felt foolish asking, but he'd been attacked by an unreasonable fit of jealousy. 'Married couples?'

'Chris is a bachelor,' she said in a matter of fact tone. Her eyes were defiant as she looked at him. 'Leanne and

Tim are married. If I have time later today I'll phone around and send out a few feelers.'

'I think that's wise.'

Lucy concentrated on piling tomatoes onto her fork. She looked upset and they finished their breakfast in uncomfortable silence.

Will felt upset too, but he wasn't sure why. He and Lucy had achieved their goal and now they were moving onto the next stage of their plan. She was going to be a single mum and he was going to visit their child from time to time.

That was what he wanted, wasn't it? Fatherhood without strings. He should have been on top of the world.

From the start he'd said that he would remain an outsider in their child's life. The silent scream inside him didn't make sense.

He heard the sound of a car pulling up and a door slamming.

'That's Jane, my assistant, ready to start work,' Lucy said pointedly.

Will got to his feet. 'I'd better get out of your way.' He indicated the breakfast dishes. 'Can I help with these?'

'No, don't worry.'

She walked with him to the front door and waved to her assistant, who was using a side gate to reach the surgery. 'I'll be there in a minute, Jane,' she called.

'Don't hurry,' Jane called back, smiling broadly when she saw Will.

Lucy looked unhappy. 'Make sure you come and see me before you go,' she told him.

'Yes, of course.'

Her mouth trembled and she blinked.

He said inadequately, 'Thanks for breakfast.' And then he dipped his head and kissed her cheek.

Lucy mumbled something about a very busy day, gave him a brief wave and shut the door.

After Will left, her day proved to be even busier than she'd expected but, every so often as she worked, she would remember.

I'm pregnant.

Excitement fizzed inside her and she hugged herself in secret glee. She'd been waiting for this for so long. She couldn't help thinking about all those busy little cells inside her, forming their baby.

Their baby.

Wow.

There was no time to celebrate, however. As well as her usual line-up of patients, she had to perform emergency surgery on an elderly dog and she found the work unusually stressful. She was very fond of this sweet black and white cocker spaniel. He'd been one of her first patients when she'd started working in Willowbank.

She would do what she could for him now, but she feared he was nearing the end of his days. His owner would be distraught when his time was up.

If that wasn't enough to dampen Lucy's spirits, she was upset about Will. She couldn't stop thinking about him, felt utterly miserable about him going away.

Again.

How could she bear it?

The threat of his impending departure had made her snappy with him this morning and she felt bad about that, after he'd been so excited. But how could she not be upset by the thought of saying goodbye?

She loved Will.

Letting him go felt like cutting out a vital organ. Whenever she pictured him leaving, she grew angry again. How could Will pretend to be terribly concerned about her and then take off to the wilds of a New Guinea jungle?

How could he leave her so soon? So easily?

All day, her mind churned with things she wished she'd asked him, as well as things she wished she'd told him. But the crux of her message was hard to admit—their friendship plan was a farce.

It was rubbish.

Sharing responsibility for a child required a commitment that went way beyond friendship.

And she and Will had already shared a beautiful intimacy that she could never classify as friendship.

Maybe it was easier for guys to be interested in sex without actually being in love, but she'd never been brave enough to be honest with Will about her feelings, so wasn't it possible that he'd hidden some of his feelings, too?

Should she try to find out?

It was crazy that she was still afraid to admit the truth about her feelings. She'd always been so worried that her disclosure might shock him, that she might alienate him completely. But today she felt different.

Determined.

She'd been hiding behind fear for too long. She was going to be a mother now and that required courage.

For her baby's sake, she should tell Will how she really felt and then face the consequences bravely.

Her confession might not make any difference. There was a chance it could make everything worse but, as the day wore on, Lucy became surer and surer that it was time to take the risk she'd shied away from for too long.

At lunch time Gina popped her head around the surgery door, her dark eyes brimming with curiosity. 'Mum's minding the twins while I do my shopping, so I thought I'd duck in quickly to see how you're going.'

'You must have a sixth sense about these things,' Lucy said, smiling.

Gina's eyes widened.

'Come and have a cuppa.' Lucy took her through to the kitchen.

'Do you have some news?' Gina asked as soon as the door that linked back to Lucy's office was firmly shut.

'I only found out this morning.'

'That you're pregnant?'

Lucy couldn't hold back her grin. 'Yes.'

Gina squealed and knocked over a kitchen chair in her rush to hug her friend. 'Oh, Lucy, I'm so excited for you.'

'I know. It's fantastic, isn't it? I have to keep pinching myself.'

'Our babies are going to be cousins,' Gina gushed.

Lucy smiled again, but this time there wasn't much joy behind it.

'I'm assuming that Will is the father,' Gina said less certainly.

'Yes, he is, and he knows about the baby. But I haven't told anyone else yet, so keep it under your hat.'

'Of course.'

The kettle came to the boil and Lucy was aware of Gina's thoughtful gaze as she poured hot water over the teabags.

'So how are things between you and Will?' she cautiously asked as Lucy handed her a mug.

'Hunky-dory.'

'Oh. That doesn't sound too promising.' Gina took a sip of tea. 'I suppose Will hasn't admitted that he loves you.'

Lucy felt the colour rush from her face. 'Don't talk nonsense, Gina. He doesn't love me.'

'Do you really believe that?'

'Yes. He can't love me. If he did, he wouldn't be taking off for PNG.'

Gina sighed. 'Is he really going away again?'

'Yes.'

'Sometimes I could wring his neck.'

'He's the man he is,' Lucy said, surprised that she could sound philosophical about a sad fact that was breaking her heart. 'Everyone in Willowbank knows Will doesn't belong here.'

'I'm not so sure about that, actually. But, anyway, he could always take you with him when he goes away.'

'I can't take off for some remote mining site when I'm pregnant. I certainly couldn't live there with a tiny baby.'

'Well…no. I don't suppose you could.' Gina gritted her teeth. 'So, do you need me to wring my brother's neck or try to hammer some sense into him?'

'No,' said Lucy, crossing her fingers behind her back. 'Leave it to me.'

By mid-afternoon the pace in the surgery wasn't quite so hectic and Lucy sent her father a text message:

Are you busy? Can I phone you?

The two of them had always been good mates and she wanted him to know her news.

Almost immediately, he called her back. 'Darling, I have five minutes. What can I do for you?'

'I just wanted to share some good news, Dad. I'm pregnant.'

She waited for his shocked gasp, but he surprised her. 'That's wonderful news. Congratulations.'

'Really, Dad? You don't mind?'

'Do *you* mind, Lucy?'

'No. I'm actually very, very happy.'

'Then so am I. I'm delighted. Couldn't be happier.'

Lucy was amazed that he didn't immediately bombard her with predictable questions about the baby's father, or when she was planning to be married.

Her dad simply asked, 'Are you keeping well?'

She grinned. First and last, Alistair McKenty was a doctor. 'It's very early days, but I'm feeling fine. I have good vibes about this pregnancy.'

'You'll see Ken Harper?'

'Yes, Dad.' Ken Harper was Willowbank Hospital's only obstetrician. 'And, as you know, Ken will give me top antenatal care.'

She heard a chuckle on the other end of the line and she waited for more questions. When there was silence, she said, 'In case you were wondering, Will Carruthers is the baby's father.'

'Ah.'

'Ah? What does that mean?'

'I noticed that Will's been home for rather longer than usual.'

Heat suffused Lucy. 'Is that all you can say?'

'No. I'm actually very pleased. I like Will. I always expected you two to get together.'

'You did?'

'You used to be such terrific friends, but then you took up with that older brother.'

'Yes.'

'I never understood that, Lucy. Josh Carruthers had girl-friends all over the district.'

'Dad, I don't really want to go back over that now.'

'I'm sorry. You're right. It's all in the past.'

'Actually, there is one thing about that time I've been meaning to ask you.'

'What's that, dear?'

'Why didn't you tell me that Will telephoned and tried to visit me after Josh died?'

A sigh shuddered down the phone line. 'You were so distressed, Lucy, and I was upset too. Your mother wasn't around to advise, and I suppose I went into over-protective mode.'

'But Will was my friend.'

'I know, dear. I'm sorry, but I did what I thought was right. Mattie was there almost every day, and she was a huge help. And, to be honest, Will wasn't his normal self at the time. He was acting quite strangely. Extremely tense. Distraught, actually. I didn't see how he could do you any good.'

Lucy pressed two fingers to the bridge of her nose to hold back the threat of tears. She knew there was no point in getting upset about this. It wasn't her father's fault that Will had taken off again, without leaving her any hint that he'd wanted to keep in touch.

It wasn't her father's fault that her own feelings of guilt had driven her to silence, adding more strain to an already tense friendship.

'Well, things are still complicated between Will and me,' she admitted.

'Is he planning to continue working overseas?'

'Yes.'

'How do you feel about that?'

'OK.' Lucy forced a smile into her voice. 'It's what we planned.'

'So this baby was planned?'

'Yes. Will and I decided we'd like to have a baby together, but we'll just remain friends.'

There was a significant pause. 'Are you really happy with that arrangement, Lucy?'

She couldn't give a direct answer. 'Dad, I knew what Will was like when we started talking about this.'

There was another sigh on the other end of the line. Another pause. 'My big concern is that you must look after yourself.'

'I will, Dad. I promise.'

'I'm afraid I have to go now. Come and see me soon. Come for dinner.'

'I will. Thanks. Love you, Dad.'

Lucy was about to disconnect when her father spoke again. 'Lucy.'

The tone of his voice made her grip the phone more tightly. 'Yes?'

'I've always thought that if two very good friends fall in love, they should grab their good luck with both hands.'

Lucy couldn't think of anything to say.

'It's the greatest happiness this life can offer,' her father said.

And then he hung up.

CHAPTER TEN

IT HAD been a long hot day and a summer storm broke late in the afternoon. By the time Lucy closed up the surgery, it was raining and thunder rumbled in the distance.

It was still raining heavily half an hour later when she set out for Tambaroora. She was nervous, but she was determined to see Will this evening before she chickened out again.

It wasn't yet six but the sky was already dark and her windscreen wipers had to work overtime. The winding, unsealed country roads had quickly turned to slippery mud so, despite her impatience, she had to drive very slowly and carefully.

She could see wet sheep clustered beneath the inadequate shelter of skinny gum trees. Thunder rolled all around the valley and white flashes of sheet lightning lit the entire sky. She was relieved when she finally saw the lights of Tambaroora homestead.

As soon as she pulled up at the bottom of the front steps she made a dash for the veranda.

Will's mother, wearing an apron, greeted Lucy warmly and she could smell the tempting aroma of dinner cooking. 'You were brave to come out in this terrible storm,' she said.

'I know it's not a good time to be calling, but I was hoping to see Will.'

Jessie Carruthers smiled. 'He's told us your news.'

'Are you pleased?' Lucy asked.

'Very,' Jessie said. 'Especially when Will told us that you were so happy about it.'

Lucy held her breath, wondering if Jessie would make a reference to her previous pregnancy with her elder son. But she said simply, 'Will and his father have spent the whole afternoon out in the shed, working on the tractor.' She smiled. 'You know what boys are like with their toys.'

'You must be pleased that Will's taking an interest.'

'Well, yes, I am, actually, and he's still at it. Robert came back a few minutes ago and he's in the shower. But Will's still out there, tinkering away.'

'I'll drive over and see if I can find him.'

'All right, love.' Jessie gave a wistful sigh. 'I suppose you're as disappointed as I am that Will's going away again so soon.'

'Well…I'm not surprised.'

'You might be able to talk him out of it, Lucy.'

Lucy stared at Will's mother, surprised. 'I could try, I guess. But I'm afraid it might be like trying to persuade a leopard to change his spots.'

Jessie frowned. 'I don't understand young people these days.'

'I'm not sure that we understand ourselves,' Lucy admitted.

Jessie accepted this with a resigned shrug. 'Anyway, it's lovely to see you, dear. And you must join us for dinner.'

Lucy thanked her and then drove her ute around to the back of the house, past garden beds filled with blue hydrangeas and a vegetable plot where tomatoes and fennel and silverbeet had been drenched by the heavy rain.

From there, she went through a gate, then followed muddy wheel tracks across a wet paddock till she reached the old galvanised iron structure that served as a machinery shed.

There was a light inside the shed and her heart was as fluttery as a bird's as she turned off her ute's motor. Consciously gathering her courage, she hurried to the lighted doorway.

The rain was making a dreadful racket on the iron roof so there was no point in knocking. She went inside and the smell of diesel oil seemed to close in around her. The shed was almost a museum of ageing tractors and the walls were hung with relics from the past—an ancient riding harness, the metal steps of a sulky, even a wagon wheel.

She saw the top of Will's head as he bent over a modern tractor engine, tapping at it with a spanner.

The storm battered against the iron walls and Lucy began to wonder why she'd thought it was so important to hurry over here. She'd never seen Will working at any kind of mechanical task and she felt like an intruder. He was probably trying to get the job finished by dinner time and he might not appreciate her interruption.

'Will,' she called.

He looked up and his eyebrows lifted with surprise. 'Lucy, what are you doing here?'

Setting down the spanner, he grabbed at a rag and wiped his hands as he hurried around the front of the tractor.

His shoulders stretched the seams of a faded blue cotton shirt. Weather-beaten jeans rode low on his hips and everything about him looked perfect to her.

He smiled and she felt a familiar ripple of yearning, but

she felt something deeper too—the painful awareness of how very deeply she loved this man.

That love hurt.

'Is everything all right?' he asked.

'I'm fine, Will. Still pregnant.'

His face relaxed visibly.

'I needed to talk to you, but it's been a busy day. I came as soon as I could get away.'

'You should be sitting down.' He frowned as he looked about the untidy shed. 'We used to have a chair out here somewhere. Oh, there it is.'

He freed a metal chair from a tangle of tools in the corner and wiped cobwebs and dust from it with a rag. Then he carefully tested the chair's legs and, finally satisfied, he set it on the concrete floor.

Lucy thanked him and sat with necessary dignity.

She thought, for a moment, that Will would remain standing, towering over her and making her more nervous than ever, but he found a perch on the tractor's running board.

'So you've had a busy day,' he said, still wiping the last of the grease from his hands. 'Have you had time to tell anyone your good news?'

'Gina called in at lunch time and I told her about the baby. She's over the moon, of course. I rang my dad, and I spoke to your mother just now. Everyone seems really pleased.'

She dropped her gaze to her hands, clenched white-knuckled in her lap. 'But they're all a little mystified when they realise you're still going away, Will. Somehow we're going to have to explain our arrangement to them. They need to understand we won't be living together as traditional parents.'

She wished she didn't feel so sick and nervous. Outside, a gust of wind caught a metal door, slamming it against the shed wall.

'Actually, I've changed my mind about going away.'

Lucy's head snapped up and she stared at him. Her heart hammered and she wasn't sure she could trust what she'd heard.

'I've rung the PNG mining company,' he said. 'It's all arranged. I'm not going.'

'But I've just spoken to your mother and she—'

'Mum doesn't know about it yet. My father should be telling her right now.'

'Oh? I…I see.'

She felt faint. Dizzy.

'I've spent most of the afternoon talking about it with my father,' Will said, 'and it's all planned. I'm going to take care of this place, while Dad takes Mum on the trip of a lifetime to Europe.'

Oh…so his reason for staying had nothing to do with her or the baby.

Lucy tried to swallow her disappointment. 'Your mother will love that,' she said. 'I heard her plying Mattie with questions about Italy at the christening. She's dying to go overseas.'

The faintest of smiles glimmered in his eyes. 'And I don't want to be too far away from you.'

Lucy's heart leapt like an over-eager puppy, bouncing with too much excitement.

'I need to keep an eye on you now,' he said.

'I see.' She twisted her hands in her lap, hating the re-alisation that at any minute now she might burst into tears from tension.

'I want to court you.'

'Court me?'

Lucy was sure she'd misheard Will, but then she saw a flush creeping upwards from his shirt collar.

'I thought that perhaps we should go out on dates like other couples,' he said. 'To find out—'

He stopped, as if he was searching for the right words.

'To find out if we can fall in love?' Lucy supplied in a cold little voice she hardly recognised.

'Yes,' he said, clearly grateful that she understood.

Lucy was devastated. She was fighting to breathe. Will had been her friend since high school. For heaven's sake, he'd slept with her on two occasions. He was the father of her baby, and yet he still needed to take her out on dates to find out if he loved her.

A cruel icy hand squeezed around her heart.

'I really don't think dating would work,' she said, miserably aware that her life and her silly dreams were falling to pieces. 'If you were ever going to fall in love with me, it would have happened by now.'

'But, Lucy, I—'

'No!' she cried and the word sounded as if it had been ripped from her.

She held up her hands to stop him. 'I'm an expert when it comes to falling in love, Will.' Despair launched her to her feet.

Will's face was as pained as it was puzzled. He stood too.

Tears clogged Lucy's throat and she gulped to force them down. 'I know all about trying to manipulate love.'

'What do you mean?'

She saw the colour flee from Will's face and for a moment she almost retreated. Why should she force Will to hear her confession?

He wasn't going to PNG any more. Perhaps that was enough. She should be grateful for small mercies.

But no, she'd promised herself that she wouldn't be a coward. Will was, after all, her baby's father. Her confession wouldn't change that.

She took a deep breath and dived in. 'I tried to make you fall in love with me once before, Will, but it didn't work.'

Dismayed, he shook his head. 'I don't understand.'

'I'm telling you something rather terrible, actually.' She fixed her gaze on a huge muddy tractor tyre. 'I started going out with Josh because I was hoping you'd hear about it and be jealous.'

She heard the shocked sound Will made, but she couldn't look at him.

'My plan backfired,' she said. 'Josh was more than I'd bargained for.' Her cheeks flamed. 'Then I discovered I was pregnant.'

Shyly, she lifted her gaze.

Will's eyes were wild, but he held himself very still, hands fisted. 'Please tell me that Josh didn't force you.'

'No, he didn't use force, but I was young and he was very persuasive.'

A harsh sound escaped him. He began to pace, but then he whirled around to face her. 'Is that why you became engaged to Josh? Because you found out you were pregnant?'

'Yes.' Tears spilled suddenly.

Tears of shame.

And relief.

It was so good to have her confession out in the open at last.

'I was such an idiot, Will, and I ended up being trapped by my mistakes.'

'Goose.' With a choked cry, Will closed the gap between them, pulling her roughly into his arms. 'I thought you were in love with Josh.'

She shook her head and pressed her damp face into the curve of his neck.

A groan broke from him. He enfolded her against the wonderful warmth and strength of his chest and she could feel his heart knocking against hers.

'I was so angry with Josh,' he said. 'I was scared he wouldn't love you enough. Scared he wouldn't try hard enough to make you happy and keep you happy.'

'Oh, Will.'

'We had a terrible row just before he took off in the plane.'

Lucy leaned back and looked up at him, saw horror and tenderness warring in his eyes. 'How awful.'

'I still feel sick every time I think of it.'

'That's a terrible burden to have carried all these years.'

'Yes. I've blamed myself for a long time.'

She wanted to ease the pain in his eyes. 'But it wasn't your fault. Josh always made his own decisions.'

He nodded sadly. 'Short of holding a gun to his head, I couldn't have stopped him.'

Lucy shivered and took a step out of the comforting circle of Will's arms. She thought about the way that one event had shaped their lives. Wished that her confession had brought her a sense of peace.

It would be too much to expect a similar avowal of love from Will.

'It was nice of you to offer to court me,' she said and she pressed a fist against her aching heart, as if somehow she could stop it from bleeding. 'But if you don't mind, I think I'd rather not go on those dates.'

'But—' Will began.

Lucy hurried on. 'I think it would be better if we stick to friendship.'

'Why?'

Why? How could he ask that? After everything he'd had to say on the subject of friendship.

Lucy gave a shrug of annoyance. 'We've managed very well as friends for a long time now.'

'But you said you loved me.'

Oh, God.

Her heart stopped.

Will sent her a bewildered little smile. 'You don't have a monopoly on mistakes, Lucy.'

She felt rooted to the floor and her body flashed hot and cold. 'What do you mean? Have you made mistakes?'

His smile tilted with faint irony. 'Self delusion tops my list.'

Tears burned her eyes but she dashed them away because she wanted to see the raw emotion in Will's face. She'd never seen anything more beautiful.

'I've always cared about you, Lucy. I've always wanted to make you happy, but somehow—' He gave a sad shake of his head. 'Some *crazy* how—I couldn't see what that caring really meant.'

His eyes shimmered brightly. 'I made my first terrible mistake when you kissed me goodbye.' He reached for her hand. 'That was the kiss to end all kisses. I should have bound you to my side and never let you out of my sight. Instead, I was a fool, and I took off overseas.'

'I didn't know you liked that kiss,' she whispered.

He gave an abrupt laugh. 'I tried to tell myself I'd read

it wrongly. That maybe you were a particularly talented kisser, and that you kissed everyone that fabulously.'

'Not a chance, Will.'

'I spent far too much time on that first trip trying to forget you.' He tucked a curl behind her ear. 'I think that was about mistake number thirty-three.'

Lucy could hear the frantic beating of her heart and she realised the rain and the wind had stopped. 'Were there any more mistakes?'

'Dozens,' he admitted with a rueful smile. 'Every time I talked to you about friendship I was being an idiot.'

She felt the warmth of his fingers stroking her cheek. He touched her chin, lifted her face so that she was lost in the silver of his eyes. 'We should have been talking about love, Lucy.'

She couldn't speak.

'I love you,' he said again, and she tried to smile but she sobbed instead.

'I love you, Goose.'

Will kissed her damp eyelashes. 'You're the most important person in the world to me. That's got to be love, hasn't it?'

She could feel a smile growing inside her. 'It does sound promising.'

His eyes shone. 'I want to protect you and your baby.'

'Our baby,' Lucy corrected, and yes, she was definitely smiling on the outside now.

'I want to make you happy every day. I want to sleep with you every night and have breakfast with you every morning.'

'That definitely sounds like more than friendship, Will.' Smiling widely, she reached up and touched the grainy skin of his jaw. 'And I should know. I've loved you for so long I don't know any other way to be.'

His hands framed her face and his eyes were shining. With love. 'Do you think you could marry me, Lucy?'

She smiled as a fleeting memory from a time long ago flitted through her mind—pages of a school book filled with her handwriting: *Lucy Carruthers. Mrs Lucy Carruthers.*

'I'd love to marry you, Will.'

He punched the air and let out a war whoop. 'Sorry,' he said, 'but I couldn't help it. I just feel so damn happy.'

And then Will kissed her.

He poured his happiness and his love and his soul into the kiss and Lucy discovered that an old shed with a leaky roof was the most romantic place in the world.

CHAPTER ELEVEN

THEIR baby chose to be born on a crisp clear winter's day in July.

Will rose early when it was still dark. He built up the fire in the living room so it could heat the whole house and, with that task completed, he returned briefly to his bedroom doorway. He smiled at the sight of Lucy still sleeping, the tips of her blonde curls just showing above the warm duvet.

He continued on to the back door, donned a thick, fleecy lined coat and heavy boots and went out into the frosty dawn to the first of his daily tasks—checking the condition of the pregnant ewes and any lambs born during the night.

The sun was a pale glimmer on the distant horizon and the sky was grey and bleak, his breath a white cloud. Grass underfoot was crisp with frost. Last week he'd started spreading hay and feeding their flock with winter grain stored in their silos.

Farming was constant work, but Will loved his new life. Loved being in the outdoors, loved working with the animals and the land, planning the seasonal calendar of tasks required to keep the business running smoothly.

Best of all, he loved sharing every aspect of farm life with Lucy.

His wife was a walking encyclopaedia when it came to sheep and there'd been plenty of times when he'd had to humbly ask for her advice. But lately Lucy had been endearingly absent-minded, her attention turning more and more frequently inward to their baby.

And that was the other grand thing about Will's life these days—the pregnancy.

Of all the adventures he'd enjoyed, this surely had to be the greatest. Will never tired of watching the happy light in Lucy's eyes, or the proud way she carried herself as their baby grew and grew. Never tired of seeing the baby's movements ripple across her belly, or feeling stronger and stronger kicks beneath his hand.

Together Will and Lucy had converted his old bedroom into a sunny nursery, with yellow walls and bright curtains and a farmyard frieze.

'The kid will only have to look out the window to see a farmyard,' Will had teased.

But Lucy wanted farm animals so that was what they had, along with a wicker rocking chair and a fitted carpet, a handmade quilt lovingly pieced by his mother, as well as a white cot with a soft lamb's wool rug.

And any day their baby would arrive and they'd be a family.

At last.

This morning, Will refilled the water troughs and pulled down extra bales of hay which he spread for the pregnant ewes, and he checked the three healthy lambs that had been born overnight.

Satisfied that all was well, he returned to the warm

kitchen, ready for breakfast, and found Lucy already up and busy at the stove. His heart lifted as it always did when he saw her.

She was wearing one of his baggy old football jerseys—blue and yellow stripes—over blue maternity jeans and her feet were encased in fluffy slippers.

'Hey there,' she said, turning to smile as he entered.

He came up behind her, slipped his arms around her and kissed her just below the ear. 'How's my favourite farmer's wife?'

'Fat, pregnant and in the kitchen.' Lucy laughed as she leaned back against him and lifted her lips to kiss the underside of his jaw.

'That's exactly how I want her,' Will growled softly, dipping his lips to trap hers for a longer, deeper kiss.

When they sat down to eat, he was surprised to see that Lucy had nothing besides a mug of tea.

'Aren't you hungry?' he asked, feeling guilty that he'd already started on his mushrooms and toast.

She smiled and shook her head.

'That's not like you.'

'It's just a precaution.'

He felt a stab of alarm. 'A precaution?'

'I've been having contractions.'

Will almost choked on his food. 'Lucy. My God, what are you doing, sitting here watching me eat breakfast? I've got to get you to hospital.'

'It's OK, Will. There's no rush.' She smiled at his dismay. 'The contractions are still twenty minutes apart.'

'Twenty minutes?' He couldn't have been gone much longer than twenty minutes. 'How many have you had? When did they start?'

'They began around four this morning.' She must have seen the panic in his face and she laughed. 'Don't worry. With a first baby it might take ages. I could go on like this all day.'

'But you might not. And it's a good hour's drive to the hospital.' How could she sit there looking so calm? Was she crazy? 'Shouldn't you ring the doctor?'

Lucy nodded. 'I'll ring him when I'm certain that it's not a false—'

She didn't finish the sentence. Without warning, her entire manner changed. She sat very still, her face concentrated. Inward. Breathing steadily but deeply. In, out. In, out.

Nervously, Will watched his wife. If Lucy was in labour he wanted her safely in hospital, surrounded by a team of medical experts.

'Phew,' she said at last. 'That was stronger.'

'What about the timing? How far was it from the last one?'

She looked at the clock. 'Gosh, it was only ten minutes.'

'That's it then.' Will lurched to his feet. 'Come on, we've got to leave *now*.'

Lucy caught his hand. 'Are you sure you don't want your breakfast?'

'Not now.'

Lucy's suitcase had been packed and ready for some weeks. 'I'll put your bag in the car,' he said, grateful that they'd bought a comfortable all wheel drive station wagon some months back.

'OK. I'd better get the rest of my things.'

He gave her a tremulous smile, but there was nothing tremulous about Lucy's grin. Her face was alight with exhilaration. 'Isn't this exciting, Will? Our baby's coming.'

A tidal wave of emotions flooded him. Glorious love for

her. Chilling fear and a desperate need to protect her. Closing the gap between them, Will took her in his arms. 'I love you so much.'

'I know, my darling.' She touched a gentle hand to his cheek.

He clasped her to him, his precious, precious girl. 'I'm going to get you there safely, Lucy. I promise.'

Will drove with his heart in his mouth. Despite Lucy's calm assertion that all was well, he knew her contractions were getting stronger and he suspected they seemed to be coming closer. He could tell by her bouts of deep breathing and the way she massaged her stomach and he knew she needed all her concentration just to get through the pain.

Now he cursed himself for not making better contingency plans. He'd tried to suggest that Lucy stay in town with her father for these final weeks, but she'd insisted she'd be fine. He'd read the books on childbirth. He knew every case was different. Hell, he shouldn't have listened to her.

'Sorry, this is going to be bumpy,' he said as they came to the old wooden bridge crossing Willow Creek.

'It's OK,' she said, smiling bravely. 'I'm between contractions.'

But they had only just made it to the other side of the bridge when Lucy gave a loud gasp.

'What's happening?' Will sent her a frantic sideways glance.

She couldn't answer. She was too busy panting.

Panting? Didn't that mean—?

'Lucy!' he cried, aghast. 'You're not in transition already, are you?'

'I think I might be,' she said when she'd recovered her

breath. For the first time she looked frightened. 'First babies shouldn't come this fast.'

She no longer sounded calm. All too soon, her eyes were closed, her face twisted with pain, one fist clutched low, beneath the bump of the baby.

Oh, God. They were still thirty minutes from the hospital. Will felt helpless and distraught as he pressed his foot down on the accelerator. His heart began to shred into tiny pieces.

As they rounded the next curve, Lucy cried out and the guttural animal force of the sound horrified Will. Seizing the first possible chance to pull off the road, he brought the car to a halt.

'I'll ring for an ambulance,' he said, already reaching for his mobile phone.

Lucy nodded and managed a weak smile. 'Good idea. I…I think the baby's coming.'

Will choked back a cry of dismay.

The voice on the other end of the emergency hotline was amazingly calm as he explained their situation and gave the necessary details, including their location.

'The ambulance is on its way,' he said, wishing he felt more relieved.

Lucy nodded and fumbled with her door handle.

'What are you doing?' he cried as her door swung open. Had she gone mad?

Leaping out of his seat, he hurried around the car and found his wife slumped against its side, panting furiously.

Helplessly, he tried to stroke her arm, to soothe her, but she pushed him away and shook her head. He stood beside her, scared she might collapse, arms at the ready.

When the panting was over she opened her eyes. She looked exhausted. Sweat beaded her upper lip. 'It's too painful sitting in that front seat. I think I need to get into the back.'

'Right,' he said, biting back his fear. 'Let me help you.'

He hated to see Lucy's pain as he struggled to help her with the unwieldy transfer. Her contractions were fast and furious now and there seemed to be no spaces between them. He found a cushion for her head and helped her to lie along the back seat.

In a tiny lull, she sent him a wan smile. 'I'm sorry. I didn't dream it would be this fast.'

'Our baby can't wait to get here,' he said, doing his best to sound calm. 'He knows what a great mother he's getting.'

After the next contraction Lucy said quite calmly, 'Do we have any towels? Can you get the baby blanket out of the suitcase, Will?'

The baby blanket? He must have looked shocked.

'In case we beat the ambulance,' she said.

No, no. That couldn't happen, surely?

But by the time he'd found a beach towel—freshly washed, thank God—and retrieved the baby blanket from the hospital suitcase, Lucy was panting so hard she was in danger of hyperventilating.

'It's coming!' she cried. 'Will, help me!'

With frantic hands, she was trying to push her clothing away in preparation for the baby's imminent birth.

Oh, God it was actually happening. This was it. The birth of their child. On the side of the road beneath a river red gum.

Over the past nine months Will had imagined this birth, but he'd always pictured himself watching from the side-lines while medical experts did the honours. Mostly he'd seen himself emerging from a delivery room wearing a green hospital gown and a beaming smile as he shared the good news with their waiting families.

But, to his surprise, as soon as he accepted that he had no choice about where their baby might be born, an unexpected sense of calm settled over him. The terror was still there like a savage claw in the pit of his stomach, but Lucy needed him and he had to pull himself together.

Before they'd left home, he'd promised to protect her. He'd never dreamed what that might involve, but this was the moment of reckoning. She needed him to be calm and competent.

He could do this. For her. For their baby.

'OK, Goose, you're doing really well,' he said as he settled the folded towel beneath her.

Lucy merely grunted and went red in the face. Her right hand was braced against the back of the front seat. With the other she clung to an overhead strap.

She held her breath and grimaced, and Will couldn't bear to think how much this was hurting her.

Then he saw the crown of their baby's head.

Lucy finished pushing and let out an enormous gasp as she wilted back against the cushion.

'Good girl,' he said. 'Our baby has dark hair.'

She tried to smile. 'I'm going to have to push, Will. I can't hold back any longer. If you can see the baby's head, that means I can push without doing any harm.'

'Tell me what to do,' he said, ashamed of the hint of fear that trembled in his voice.

'Just be ready to catch. Support the head.' Lucy sent him an encouraging smile before her belly constricted and she was overtaken by the force of another contraction.

Inch by inch, their baby emerged.

'You're brilliant, darling,' he told her. 'I can see the eyebrows, eyes, nose.' Excitement bubbled through him now. 'I can see the mouth. It's kinda scrunched but cute.' He held his hands at the ready. 'OK, the head's out.'

Somehow he managed to sound calm. 'It's turning.'

With the next of Lucy's grunts, he gently but firmly held his child's warm damp head. He saw a slippery shoulder emerge and then another. In the space of three heartbeats, he was steadying his baby as it slipped from its safe maternal cocoon.

He and Lucy had chosen not to know the baby's sex, but now his heart leapt with incredible joy.

'Lucy, it's a boy.'

'A boy?' Her eyes opened and a radiant smile lit up her face. 'Oh, the little darling. I had a feeling he was a boy.'

Will's throat was too choked to speak as he lifted his son onto Lucy's tummy. Their son had thick dark hair, and his little arms were outstretched, tiny fingers uncurled, as if he was reaching out for life, or bursting through the winner's tape at the end of a race.

'Oh, Will!' Lucy whispered, looking pale but happy. 'Isn't he handsome? Isn't he gorgeous?'

'He looks like a champion,' Will agreed, but then he frowned as a new fear worried him. 'Should I do anything? Is he breathing OK?'

'I think he's fine.' Lucy spoke calmly as she rubbed the baby's back and, as if to answer her, the little fellow began to cry, with a small bleat at first, then with a loud gusty wail.

She grinned. 'He's got a terrific set of lungs.'

'He's got a terrific mum,' Will said as he helped her to wrap their son in the soft white blanket dotted with yellow ducklings.

The whine of a siren sounded in the distance and Will felt a weight lift from his shoulders.

'Help is on its way,' he said.

Lucy smiled. 'I've already had all the help I needed.' With a wondrous, soft expression she touched the top of their son's head. 'Thank you, Will. Thank you.'

By midday Lucy was happily ensconced in a private room in Willowbank Hospital in a lovely big white bed, with her darling baby boy, wrapped in a blue bunny rug, beside her.

Surrounded by flowers.

Surrounded by so many flowers, in fact, that she felt like a celebrity.

'You *are* a celebrity,' Gina told her. 'Think how many puppies and kittens and ponies and sheep you've looked after in this district. Every household in Willowbank is thrilled that you now have your own dear little boy.'

'And he's such a beauty,' said Mattie, gazing fondly at the sleeping little cherub in the crib.

Lucy watched the soft glow in Mattie's eyes, watched the reverent way Mattie stared at little Nathan, at the way she gently touched his cheek, and she felt a tiny current of excitement inside her.

The excitement grew as Lucy saw the meaningful glance Mattie sent to her husband, and a thrilled shiver ran through her as she witnessed the warm intimacy of Jake's answering smile.

They had important news. Baby news. Lucy could feel it in her bones.

'Mattie…' she said, but then she stopped, not sure how to continue.

Mattie smiled, almost as if she was encouraging Lucy to question her.

'You're not?' Lucy began and then she stopped again.

'Yes!' Mattie exclaimed and she was smiling broadly now. She reached for Jake's hand and their fingers twined. Her eyes glowed. 'I'm three months pregnant.'

'And we couldn't be happier,' said Jake, backing up his words with a huge grin.

The room suddenly erupted with excited questions and congratulations.

'That's the most perfect news,' Lucy said and she knew she was beaming with joy as she looked around the room, filled with the people who were so important to her—Gina and Tom, Mattie and Jake—and Will, her darling Will. And now, dear little Nathan William Carruthers.

'There's going to be a whole new generation of the Willow Creek gang,' Tom said, grinning.

Everyone laughed and, from his vantage point near the door, Will sent his wife a conspiratorial wink. He thought Lucy had never looked more beautiful.

He looked around the room at their friends and he marvelled at the sense of completion he felt. He thought about the long and roundabout journey he'd taken to reach this satisfying moment.

And he knew at last that he was finally home.

* * * * *

*Celebrate 60 years of pure reading pleasure
with Harlequin®!*

To commemorate the event, Silhouette Special
Edition invites you to Ashley O'Ballivan's bed-and-
breakfast in the small town of Stone Creek. The beautiful innkeeper will have her hands full caring for her
old flame Jack McCall. He's on the run and recovering from a mysterious illness, but that won't stop
him from trying to win Ashley back.

*Enjoy an exclusive glimpse of Linda Lael Miller's
AT HOME IN STONE CREEK
Available in November 2009
from Silhouette Special Edition®*

The helicopter swung abruptly sideways in a dizzying arch, setting Jack McCall's fever-ravaged brain spinning.

His friend's voice sounded tinny, coming through the earphones. "You belong in a hospital," he said. "Not some backwater bed-and-breakfast."

All Jack really knew about the virus raging through his system was that it wasn't contagious, and there was no known treatment for it besides a lot of rest and quiet. "I don't like hospitals," he responded, hoping he sounded like his normal self. "They're full of sick people."

Vince Griffin chuckled but it was a dry sound, rough at the edges. "What's in Stone Creek, Arizona?" he asked. "Besides a whole lot of nothin'?"

Ashley O'Ballivan was in Stone Creek, and she was a whole lot of somethin', but Jack had neither the strength nor the inclination to explain. After the way he'd ducked out six months before, he didn't expect a welcome, knew he didn't deserve one. But Ashley, being Ashley, would take him in whatever her misgivings.

He had to get to Ashley; he'd be all right.

He closed his eyes, letting the fever swallow him.

There was no telling how much time had passed when he became aware of the chopper blades slowing overhead. Dimly, he saw the private ambulance waiting on the airfield outside of Stone Creek; it seemed that twilight had descended.

Jack sighed with relief. His clothes felt clammy against his flesh. His teeth began to chatter as two figures unloaded a gurney from the back of the ambulance and waited for the blades to stop.

"Great," Vince remarked, unsnapping his seat belt. "Those two look like volunteers, not real EMTs."

The chopper bounced sickeningly on its runners, and Vince, with a shake of his head, pushed open his door and jumped to the ground, head down.

Jack waited, wondering if he'd be able to stand on his own. After fumbling unsuccessfully with the buckle on his seat belt, he decided not.

When it was safe the EMTs approached, following Vince, who opened Jack's door.

His old friend Tanner Quinn stepped around Vince, his grin not quite reaching his eyes.

"You look like hell warmed over," he told Jack cheerfully.

"Since when are you an EMT?" Jack retorted.

Tanner reached in, wedged a shoulder under Jack's right arm and hauled him out of the chopper. His knees immediately buckled, and Vince stepped up, supporting him on the other side.

"In a place like Stone Creek," Tanner replied, "everybody helps out."

They reached the wheeled gurney, and Jack found himself on his back.

Tanner and the second man strapped him down, a process that brought back a few bad memories.

"Is there even a hospital in this place?" Vince asked irritably from somewhere in the night.

"There's a pretty good clinic over in Indian Rock," Tanner answered easily, "and it isn't far to Flagstaff." He paused to help his buddy hoist Jack and the gurney into the back of the ambulance. "You're in good hands, Jack. My wife is the best veterinarian in the state."

Jack laughed raggedly at that.

Vince muttered a curse.

Tanner climbed into the back beside him, perched on some kind of fold-down seat. The other man shut the doors.

"You in any pain?" Tanner said as his partner climbed into the driver's seat and started the engine.

"No." Jack looked up at his oldest and closest friend and wished he'd listened to Vince. Ever since he'd come down with the virus—a week after snatching a five-year-old girl back from her non-custodial parent, a small-time Colombian drug dealer—he hadn't been able to think about anyone or anything but Ashley. When he *could* think, anyway.

Now, in one of the first clearheaded moments he'd experienced since checking himself out of Bethesda the day before, he realized he might be making a major mistake. Not by facing Ashley—he owed her that much and a lot more. No, he could be putting her in danger, putting Tanner and his daughter and his pregnant wife in danger, too.

"I shouldn't have come here," he said, keeping his voice low.

Tanner shook his head, his jaw clamped down hard as though he was irritated by Jack's statement.

"This is where you belong," Tanner insisted. "If you'd had sense enough to know that six months ago, old buddy, when you bailed on Ashley without so much as a fare-thee-well, you wouldn't be in this mess."

Ashley. The name had run through his mind a million times in those six months, but hearing somebody say it out loud was like having a fist close around his insides and squeeze hard.

Jack couldn't speak.

Tanner didn't press for further conversation.

The ambulance bumped over country roads, finally hitting smooth blacktop.

"Here we are," Tanner said. "Ashley's place."

* * * * *

Will Jack be able to patch things up with Ashley,
or will his past put the woman he loves in harm's way?
Find out in
AT HOME IN STONE CREEK
by Linda Lael Miller
Available November 2009
from Silhouette Special Edition®

**This November,
Silhouette Special Edition®
brings you**

NEW YORK TIMES
BESTSELLING AUTHOR

LINDA LAEL
MILLER

At Home in
Stone Creek

*Available in November
wherever books are sold.*

HARLEQUIN Romance®

This November,
queen of the rugged rancher

PATRICIA THAYER

teams up with

DONNA ALWARD

*to bring you an extra-special treat
this holiday season—*

two romantic stories
in one book!

Join sisters Amelia and Kelley for Christmas at
Rocking H Ranch where these feisty cowgirls swap
presents for proposals, mistletoe for marriage and
experience the unbeatable rush of falling in love!

Available in November wherever books are sold.

www.eHarlequin.com

HR17619

REQUEST YOUR FREE BOOKS!
2 FREE NOVELS PLUS 2
FREE GIFTS!

HARLEQUIN®

Romance®

From the Heart, For the Heart

YES! Please send me 2 FREE Harlequin® Romance novels and my 2 FREE gifts (gifts are worth about $10). After receiving them, if I don't wish to receive any more books, I can return the shipping statement marked "cancel". If I don't cancel, I will receive 4 brand-new novels every month and be billed just $3.84 per book in the U.S. or $4.24 per book in Canada. That's a savings of at least 15% off the cover price! It's quite a bargain! Shipping and handling is just 50¢ per book.* I understand that accepting the 2 free books and gifts places me under no obligation to buy anything. I can always return a shipment and cancel at any time. Even if I never buy another book, the two free books and gifts are mine to keep forever.

114 HDN EYU3 314 HDN EYKG

Name	(PLEASE PRINT)	
Address		Apt. #
City	State/Prov.	Zip/Postal Code

Signature (if under 18, a parent or guardian must sign)

Mail to the **Harlequin Reader Service:**
IN U.S.A.: P.O. Box 1867, Buffalo, NY 14240-1867
IN CANADA: P.O. Box 609, Fort Erie, Ontario L2A 5X3

Not valid to current subscribers of Harlequin Romance books.

**Are you a subscriber of Harlequin Romance books
and want to receive the larger-print edition?
Call 1-800-873-8635 today!**

* Terms and prices subject to change without notice. Prices do not include applicable taxes. Sales tax applicable in N.Y. Canadian residents will be charged applicable provincial taxes and GST. Offer not valid in Quebec. This offer is limited to one order per household. All orders subject to approval. Credit or debit balances in a customer's account(s) may be offset by any other outstanding balance owed by or to the customer. Please allow 4 to 6 weeks for delivery. Offer available while quantities last.

Your Privacy: Harlequin Books is committed to protecting your privacy. Our Privacy Policy is available online at www.eHarlequin.com or upon request from the Reader Service. From time to time we make our lists of customers available to reputable third parties who may have a product or service of interest to you. If you would prefer we not share your name and address, please check here. ☐

HR09R

HARLEQUIN *Romance*®

Coming Next Month

Available November 10, 2009

For an early surprise this Christmas don't look under the
Christmas tree or in your stocking—look out for
Christmas Treats in your November Harlequin® Romance novels!

#4129 MONTANA, MISTLETOE, MARRIAGE
Christmas Treats
Patricia Thayer and Donna Alward
Join sisters Amelia and Kelley for Christmas on Rocking H Ranch as we
bring you two stories in one volume for double the romance!

#4130 THE MAGIC OF A FAMILY CHRISTMAS Susan Meier
Christmas Treats
All six-year-old Harry wants for Christmas is for his new mom, Wendy, to
marry so they can be a forever family. Will his wish come true?

#4131 CROWNED: THE PALACE NANNY Marion Lennox
Marrying His Majesty
When powerful prince Stefanos meets feisty nanny Elsa, sparks fly!
But will she ever agree to *Marrying His Majesty?* Find out in the final
installment of this majestic trilogy.

#4132 CHRISTMAS ANGEL FOR THE BILLIONAIRE Liz Fielding
Trading Places
Lady Rosanne Napier is *Trading Places* with a celebrity look-alike to
escape the spotlight and meets the man of her dreams in the start of
this brand-new duet.

#4133 COWBOY DADDY, JINGLE-BELL BABY Linda Goodnight
Christmas Treats
On a dusty Texas roadside, cowboy Dax delivers Jenna's baby. When he
offers her a job, neither expects her to become his housekeeper bride!

UNDER THE BOSS'S MISTLETOE Jessica Hart
Treats
ined to ignore the attraction she felt for her new boss,
was forced to pose under the mistletoe with